T0208907

BEYOND THE CALLA NEPTUNE

RS CANNAN

authorHOUSE°

AuthorHouse™
1663 Liberty Drive
Bloomington, IN 47403
www.authorhouse.com
Phone: 1 (800) 839-8640

Interior Graphics/Art Credit: Rebecca DeMarle

Published by AuthorHouse 04/18/2019

ISBN: 978-1-7283-0797-8 (sc)
ISBN: 978-1-7283-0796-1 (e)

Library of Congress Control Number: 2019904290

DEDICATION

THIS BOOK IS dedicated to the friends and family that have continuously encouraged me to continue writing. This book would not have been completed and therefore the trilogy would not have been finished. Thank you all.

CONTENTS

IN THE QUARTERS OF
CAPTAIN TALLOR 5

THE ENTRANCE CHIME rings and Captain Tallor 5 answers in a strong voice "Enter" In walks Master Chief and says" Captain we've been summoned to Admiral Nellon's office immediately.' Very good; what's the rush, were still on leave and the Excalibur isn't due out of refitting for another 2 solsecs. I know sir, but things have been moved up. Have you ever heard of a Commander Risig or CommanderVolarian? "Not really Master Chief, but with all of the new promotions around it doesn't surprise me. Who are they Master Chief?" Sir Commander Risig is a female and commander Volarian used to be a Lieutenant on the old Valukrie. What does that have to do with us meeting Admiral Nellon? Rumor has its sir that they have been summoned also at the same meeting we're supposed to be at. Rumor Master Chief, you should know better than that. Where did you hear this rumor? Well sir I was at the Boar and Dragon last night checking on the crew to make

1

sure they didn't get into any trouble and I heard a cook talking about it. Master Chief, please a rumor from a cook isn't very reliable. Sir there the best nobody thinks about talking around a cook everybody thinks there deaf. I've found through my experience that rumors from the cooks are very reliable. Okay, Master Chief let me get dressed and we'll go see the Admiral. Master Chief I thought that you were searing off of the Boar and Dragon since your last incident there with some Marines. Sir, I was only doing my duty to check on the crew making sure there okay. I suppose you didn't have anything to drink? Well sir, I have to be sociable around the patrons and it isn't my fault that several of the more genial ones offered me a drink so I only had one out of kindness to the older gentlemen. I see Master Chief I'm glad that you showed some restraint this time.

Let's go we don't want to be late Master Chief have you thought anything about what you're going to do when you retire? No sir, I haven't, but I would like to find a place where I can stay warm in the colder times and cool during the warmer times with plenty of liquids to keep my innards working well. I've been giving it some thought, not very often, but more frequently lately. Sir you wouldn't know what to do with yourself if you're not running around the galaxy on a mission or whatever. I know, but it keeps nagging at me.

ADMIRAL NELLONS OFFICE
AND CONFERENCE ROOM

COME IN GENTLEMEN there's some people I would like you to meet. Admiral Nellon was tall and substantially heavier than any of the other occupants. Captain Tallor this is Commander Risig, she's the captain of the new frigate Anna Maru. Commander Risig was shorter than Captain Tallor, but filled out her well-tailored uniform nicely. Captain Tallor this is Commander Volarian captain of the Fang and this is Major Pike, he's heading up the Marine contingent the 362 Space Marine Expeditionary Force. Nice to meet all of you, this is Master Chief. Every one nodded and placed the first finger to their head. Commander Volarian was tall and fit with a light ting of brown in his skin. Major Pike was tall heavy set, not fat but very muscular with a patch over his left eye. A very formidable looking man. Please have a seat and let's get started. Were gathered here to discuss the up coming mission into the frontier. Captain Tallor will be in charge of this expedition. We are going to seek out, destroy or capture the farugie pirates. They have been raiding along the frontier border through out this section of the galaxy. There is someone else I would like to have you meet. In walked a short man in long heavy multi colored robes of very expensive regal looking material. His head was covered with a flowing cap of leather a fur like material that hid the shape of his head, but he was obviously not an Asantians. Admiral Nellon introduced him as Ambassador Iz. He was a Laurencin. A race of amphibian type of people. He walked up right on two vey strong and powerful legs, his arms were shorter, but almost as powerful, his face had a short nose that was wide and his mouth was long and had long white teeth both top and bottom. His skin was a brownish green that was a heavy scale in design, but leather like. There was no discernable tail, but he walked slightly hunched over. His feet and legs were covered in wide leather boots that came half way up is leg.

Thank you Admiral Nellon. Ladies and gentlemen please let me introduce myself. His voice was deep and sounded like he was in a barrel, but very intelligible. I am happy to be here with you and I know its quite a surprise to all of you. Please be assured that I am here on a peaceful mission and our past differences have long been forgotten. My government has contacted you in a matter of great importance. The farugie pirates have been raiding along our border or some time now and we haven't been able to stop them or find out where they come from. We have asked for your governments assistance in ridding the frontier border zone of these virulent pests. I know you probably ask why we don't just get rid of them ourselves?

Well its quite simple since the past conflicts between ourselves and our neighboring star systems we are not permitted to have any deep space capability. Therefore, we come to you asking for your assistance. We feel these rogues are going to become a threat to you as they are to us, so it's only natural threat that you would want to help us and secure your own safety for your colonies near the border with the frontier. Are there any other questions? Admiral Nellon would you like to say a few words. Yes, thank you ambassador. Captain Tallor you will lead the expedition with the Annu Maru and the Fang. Ambassador Iz will accompany you on the Excalibur.

Admiral this is going to be a dangerous mission and I don't think a person of the ambassador's rank should be put in danger. We have never sent a manned mission into the frontier and we really don't know the risks and travails that exist out there. I respectively wish that you would reconsider this assignment of the ambassador to the Excalibur. We are a combat ship and we aren't set up to carry passengers with the ambassadors needs and comforts. Your concerns are noted Captain, but the Excalibur is already being retrofitted to satisfy the ambassadors physical needs.

Very well then, this meeting is concluded please repair to your ships and make preparations to get under way. Captain a copy of your written orders is being prepared so there is no misunderstanding of your duties. You will also be given a written order of search and seizure from the Galactic Court to cover any legal issues of going into the frontier in an armed ship. They will also include warrants for the arrests and detention of any pirates that you should encounter and capture. They should be brought before the court for trial on piracy charges. Very well Admiral, what are our rules of engagement? Captain you can and will use any force necessary to capture and kill any pirates you encounter.

Every one gets up and prepares to leave. Oh, Captain before I forget the Terra Forma guild has asked that we keep any eye out for one of there colonies. It seems that they haven't heard from them in a while. Admiral are they in the frontier. I don't know and I rather doubt that the guild knows either. It's just a courtesy that I'm giving them to have any of our vessels keep any eye out for them. You know haw they are, very secretive they are, about where their people go and what they do. Aye sir we'll keep a weather eye out. Good hunting captain and safe journeys.

WALKING TO THE SHUTTLE
BAY FOR TRANSPORT
TO SPACE DOCK

CAPTAIN THIS IS quit and honor to accompany you to the frontier. Thank you commander Risig. Where did the name of your ship come from? Annu Maru is from the old language it translated as the Mary Anne a long and storied name from antiquity. Since we have an all-female crew, we thought that since she's new that would be a good name for her. Did you say an all female crew Commander? Yes, we are the first in the fleet and hopefully not the last. Does it present any problems for you? No sir just the normal stress but were used to it. Our commissioning grades were the highest of any new crew, we use less fuel and less staples for a similar male dominated crew. I see Commander I look forward to working with you.

Commander Volarian how is your crew adopting to having a contingent of marines on board? Its cramped quarters sir. We were not designed for a full compliant of Marines for an extended period of time. We'll be okay once we get underway. Captain what are you expecting out there? Commander to be honest I really don't know. I think it will be a lot of nothing. There're no planets, star systems or anything that would come close to what we're used too. I'll be interested to see how the ships perform. We'll all need to keep our wits about us. And remember to make sure you have good coordinates before we enter the frontier. That's why we picked the Calla Neptune for our departure point. It's the biggest and most prominent fix we'll have, because once we enter the frontier there's no way points, or star systems that we can use for navigation. The cores should be able to keep track of the time and distance we travel.

Major Pike how are your troops doing? Very well sir there ready for a fight. Major I hope it doesn't come to that, but I feel its almost inevitable. Make sure there well briefed on our rules of engagement. I want to bring back captives not bodies. We need to get intelligence on what their plans are and how big of a force they have. I want to know their capabilities and how they think. We should do all that is possible to secure their command and control systems. We'll rendezvous at point Alpha and take our initial headings from there. Captain how long do you think we'll be gone? Ambassador I have no idea this won't be a short trip and if you have any pressing business then you should stay back. No, captain I've cleared my schedule to make this trip, but I've never been on an extended space voyage before and I don't know how I'll react. Space sickness is not rare among new crew members, just don't think about it and get into a daily routine and stick to it. Everyone boards their respective shuttle craft parked all in a row.

ABOARD THE EXCALIBUR SHUTTLE CRAFT.

MASTER CHIEF AT the helm and Captain Tallor in the copilot seat with the ambassador sitting behind in the center passenger seat. Captain I'm curious why aren't you piloting the shuttle craft? Ambassador we all have to have a certain amount of PIC time to stay qualified and so Master Chief has his turn today. I see what's PIC time. That's Pilot in Command and its regulation. Sorry for all the questions, I hope you don't get tired of them, like I said I'm new at this. Please sit back and relax and enjoy the view.

The shuttle made a long assent through the lower atmosphere and was soon traveling faster and faster to reach low orbit.

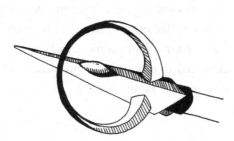

A short time later Master chief told the controllers at the space and renovation center their position and estimated time of arrival. Ambassador if you look up and forward, you'll start to seed the space dock as we come up to it. Oh, my exclaimed the ambassador as the bright shining space dock came into view. It was a huge structure like a big spider wed or cocoon that came into view. The lattice work completely surrounded a large space craft like the ambassador had never seen before. The Master Chief slowed down as he got closer. What do you think ambassador? I've never seen anything like it. Our ships are big round affairs with spikes poking out in all different directions. This is so sleek. The fuselage was long with a wide stern with large clam shell type doors open to allow the shuttle to fly right in. The long-pointed nose was flat at the tip. A large arch came up from the back and raked forward almost to the nose and completed the arch back to the other side of the stern. About a third of the way forward from the stern rose a sleek bubble that moved forward to just under the peak of the arch. The skin was a dull metallic gray color. It seems to absorb all the light around it. "That's true, but when activated it will turn into a bright shinny metallic color that blends into it's surroundings. The ship will be virtually invisible to all visual light waves and most sensor probing's. How does it do that. "that my dear ambassador is highly classified like most things on this vessel. Thank you captain I understand your position and will try not to ask anymore classified questions." No problem Ambassador I will just give you the same answer.

The shuttle swung around the stern of the ship and prepared to land. Ambassador I should warn you that when we get aboard you will probably hear a shrill whistle play a couple of notes. This is customary when a Captain or high-ranking officer comes aboard. Thank you, captain, for the warning. The shuttle slowed and gently landed about half way into the large docking bay.

ABOARD THE EXCALIBUR

THE SHUTTLE BOARDING door opened at both the top and bottom with the bottom half stairs built into it to ease stepping onto the deck. Captain Tallor exited first then the Ambassador with the Master Chief and crewman exiting last. As expected, the bosons mate piped them aboard.

The first officer approached saluted the right finger to his head and greeted everyone. "Welcome aboard the Excalibur gentlemen I hope you had an enjoyable trip. Captain Tallor introduced Ambassador Iz to the first officer and the rest of the official crew. Ambassador your personal belongings have arrived and the yeoman will escort you to your quarter. Thank you, first officer I need to refresh, myself. Captain Tallor your gear has been stowed into your stateroom. Thank you First Officer are we ready to get underway. Yes, sir just give the order. Fine let's go to the bridge and get ready. Master Chief please join us when you have things in order here. And by the way your flying skills have not deteriorated in any way since we've been back. Think you sir I'll join you shortly.

The large clam shell doors of the docking bay closed slowly and gave a loud "clank" as they locked. Let's move to the bridge so we can get underway. They climbed into the personnel lift and Captain Tallor ordered the lift to the bridge deck. As the doors opened the First Officer spoke loudly "Captain on the Deck" the bridge crew stood at attention when he entered with Ambassador Iz.

ON THE BRIDGE DECK
OF THE EXCALIBUR

AT EASE GENTLEMEN as they entered the bridge. Large expansive room with work stations laid out in a circle surrounding a raised platform. The Captain went directly to his padded metal chair suspended in the air. He announced to the deck crew "This is ambassador Iz he will be joining us on the voyage to the frontier. Please give him all due respect for him and his position. Answer his questions directly and succinctly keeping in mind he's an ambassador not a techno person." First Officer are we ready to get underway. Yes, sir on your command. Very good the command is given prepare to get underway. The captain sat down he turned to Ambassador Iz sir you may take that station over there pointing to a chair and work station to his rear and right of the rest of the work stations. Gentlemen please report your status. Each station answered in order of their position. Comm-Go, Nav-go, Sensors-go, Helm-go, Operations-go Chief Engineer-go Master Chief-go, Medical- go. Doctor welcome aboard I've never had a Medical officer before. Thank you, sir, she said, I've never been on a combat vessel before, hopefully you won't need my services. Thank you doctor, but I think there's a real good reason for your being here and I don't think it's for a free ride to the frontier. I agree sir.

Space dock control this is the Excalibur ready to leave space dock. Excalibur this is space dock control cleared to leave space dock. Cleared to Way point Alpha on your own navigation. Report visual to waypoint alpha.

Good hunting Excalibur space dock control clear Helm reverse thrusters one quarter on impulse, helm amidships, aye sir helm amidships reverse one quarter. Imperceptibly the ship started to move. The walls lite up showing the retracting gridwork outside moving away. Helm all stop, come to port ninety degrees one quarter impulse forward. The ship reacted smartly to the thruster's force and she moved to the left slowly picking up speed. She moved gracefully between two other ships waiting to dock.

Captain a quick question sir, yeas Ambassador, how do the walls light up as screens, I don't see any hardware. Sir the walls are covered with a proprietary film that acts like screens the whole ship is covered with them. If you need to see anything wherever you are in the ship just say "core show me whatever you want and it will respond to where ever you are". What about the gravity in the ship? It's all controlled by the core, the large arch you saw coming in establishes a gravitational field through out the ship. We have found by producing a field throughout that the stress on the crew is greatly diminished and allows us unlimited time in space with no ill effects. Without it all things lose body mass and bone density. You can chat with the doctor about it further if you want, but now I've got a ship to maneuver through this busy docking traffic.

Helm increase thrusters of half power on impulse. Aye sir half impulse, steady as she goes for right now. Chief engineer is the cold fusion reactor cooled enough to start generation thrust. Aye sir she's good for half-light speed on your command. Good when we leave waypoint alpha, we'll go to half light speed and then notify me when we can go to full power light speed one point six. Captain this is comm the Fang and the Mary Anne requesting ETA to waypoint Alpha. Plot put waypoint alpha up. Immediately a holographic image appeared in the center of the command circle and Captain Tallor floated up and around the image. producing a line between the image of the Excalibur and the waypoint where the two frigates awaited. They were appropriately labeled with the name and verified identification code. This image was immediately transferred to the bridges of both ships, since they all had a holographic image mode. Comm are we cinqued up with both ship in all comms and telemetry data. Yes, sir we are now we had to wait until we cleared space dock because of all the interference form the other vessels transmitting data at the same time. Good it's going to be important to keep everyone on the same page at all times especially when we get up to speed. Aye sir will do.

WAYPOINT ALPHA

CAPTAIN WE'RE APPROACHING waypoint alpha, the Fang and the Mary Anne are coming into visual range, "thanks Comm put it on visual, Aye sir" Fang and MaryAnne this is the Excalibur we have you on visual. We also have you Excalibur what a beautiful sight seeing her under power. Fang and MaryAnne we will be forming up into a standard delta formation and increasing speed to .6 light speed. Very good Captain will fall in behind you when you make your turn.

Navigation have you got the course for the Calla Neptune.? Aye sir calculated and laid in. Very good Helm come to your course for the Calla Neptune. Increase impulse speed to .6 Light speed. Aye Captain turning to our on course heading and increasing speed to .6 light speed on impulse. The Excalibur rolled slightly to starboard and gently increase speed although you couldn't feel it, just a small vibration and push back as the momentum built. Chief engineer is the reactor on line yet. Aye sir all set to go when we reach minimum velocity cooling is just about complete Helm be prepared to switch over to the main engine. Aye sir. Plot activate tactical hologram imaging. The image in the middle came into view and focused. It showed a god's eye view of the Excalibur and the two flanking frigates. All holding perfect positioning. Sir coming up to .6 light speed, very good switch over to the main engine and continue increasing speed to 1.0 light speed. Almost instantly the slight vibration diminished and a smooth increase is speed could be felt. The captain moved his chair from its locked position to floating and moving around the holographic image. Everyone was aware, but not surprised. Ambassador IZ called out, Captain what are you doing and how do you do that. Ambassador this is my standard oversight duties. My chair is fitted with an anti-gravity device that allows me to move anywhere I want. I control it by a small button, called a top hat on the arm rest. Captain is it safe to move around, yes ambassador quite safe. The ambassador went over to the walls and felt them. They were a sponge foam texture and soft to the touch. The imagery projecting on the wall was technical data from the helmsman's position. Captain why are they soft. There anti-momentum devices. It prevents you and other crewman form slamming into the wall and getting hurt or killed should we make a sudden turn or slowdown. You are traveling at the speed of light currently and if we made an abrupt maneuver you would fly all over the place and your sped is not in cinque with the ship speed. I see he said. Helm come to max cruise speed 1.6 the speed of light. Aye sir 1.6 it is. First Officer is everyone settled in and operating normally. Aye sir, very good then call officers meeting in my conference room when everyone can get here. Very good Captain should we slow down for the shuttle transfer? Negative they should be able to manage and if not then they shouldn't be flying a shuttle. Aye sir, we'll meet in your quarters.

IN THE CAPTAINS
CONFERENCE ROOM
ABOARD THE EXCALIBUR

WELL NOW EVERYONE comfortable? I believe you all know one another including Ambassador Iz. Commander Valerian and Major Pike you look a bit distressed. Yes, sir it was a rough trip over. Oh, why is that? Well sir our pilot has never made a transfer at that speed before and the gravitational wake the Excalibur leaves is something he wasn't used to or comfortable with. You didn't damage my ship, did you? No sir we just came in a little hot and had to use the emergency stopping net. Well Commander was he a Marine pilot or Space Force. Marine sir. I suggest you have him practice a bit next time. Major I suggest he catch up on his "sim" time. I will see to it sir as soon as he calms down a bit. Very good let's get started.

We will be entering the Frontier shortly and I want everyone on the same page. Plot bring up our projected course and the Calla Neptune. Aye sir. The holographic image came up. The projected course was delineated as a broken line into the frontier going about 2/3 the way through the abyss then curving to the starboard in a large curving arch back to the Calla Neptune. We will be trans versing the frontier in a delta formation. I will have all of our sensors pointed to the front and up and down. Commander Valerian you will focus your sensors to the port and behind us. Commander Risig you will be focused to the starboard back and down. This will give a 360-degree coverage spread and also on top and below us. Chief Engineer anything to add. Sir I think we will lose at least some of our power from the magneto dynamic engines once we get out of the gravitational field of our nearest stars and galaxy as a whole. No body has been out this far and I fear we will slow down. By how much Chief? Unknown sir we never experienced this before. Very good we'll watch for it. Plot- any issues. No sir we'll take a good reading on the Calla Neptune before we get out of range. Good. Navigation- none sir the core will keep us on track without a problem. Weapons-Nothing sir we should be able to handle anything or anyone we come up against. Comm-nothing sir we're all cinqued up and nothing should change that. Master Chief-nothing unusual sir all the people are ready and anxious to get to it. Last but not least doctor what have you got? Sir I've research the Farugi as much as possible and Ambassador IZ has been kind enough to give us access to all of his files. With your permission sir plot bring up my image. An image came up showing a creature on two legs stocky build with a large head and very little or no neck, He had two arms with and hazy image of two more. His mouth was large and contained large triangular teeth sharpened to a point. He had an eye in the middle top of his head and two small pointed ears on top. This is what were up against she started. There are various eye witness reports of either two arms or four arms. Neither can be verified. I assume they could be imaginations at work here also. The eye is mounted on an antennae type filament that allows him to raise it off of his head and look above and around him some say 360 degrees. Notice its one eye I think it probably has at least two lenses or possibly more to give him binocular vision. With out it he would have no depth perception like we do. They are very aggressive angered easily and violent at all occasions. They produce a clicking sound with there teeth just before they attack. I can assume this is some form of communication. There speech seems to be limited, but they might have some form of tele-communications we're not aware of. One last thing they probably have what we call double jointed hands wrists and shoulders. They are keen to get in close for combat using there sa's for slashing and dismembering their prey. I use that term because there are reports of cannibalism. Major I would take these beings as very seriously tell your men not to let them get close. Their teeth and jaws will produce very serious wounds or even take an arm or leg off. Thank you doctor we will warn them and show them your image if we get a chance to see them. They won't get that close we will destroy them at first sight. Major remember I would like prisoners if safe and possible not body count. Captain we will do our best but I will not put my men at risk just to have show trial. Major I understand and you WILL follow my directives as ordered without question. Are you onboard with that! Aye sir no disrespect intended. Good anybody else have anything they wish to add. Let's move out and continue with the mission. Captain I have a question or two, but I don't want to hold up the rest of the people. Go ahead ambassador what's your question. Sir what is the core and how does it work. Ambassador the core is the brains of the ship. It sits in the belly of the ship next to the main engine They use the same cooling system that allows us to move faster than light. We need this super-fast computing power to run everything we have. Pardon my ignorance but what is quantum computing? Our computers use the standard binary code. We need to be much faster than that and we need a huge amount of capacity. Quantum computing is like flipping a coin, you have two sides like in binary computing. With us we use the space between the front and back. This gives us huge speed advantage and shorter computing times. That's about as best of an explanation as I can give without getting into time, space and string theory. Very good Captain I'll accept you at your word.

Ambassador are your quarters comfortable for you? Yes, quite acceptable, which reminds me I need to go into the vapor and water regenerator so I can rest and be able to be my best. You know were not made for space travel, our bodily systems and functions are way off and I find as I get older, we don't function as well as we should. I understand completely we have the same problem That's why we have our lighting regulated as if we were home. Our bodily functions also suffer if we don't regenerate in our vapor chambers and take in as much water as we can. Do you recycle the water onboard? Yes, sir the environments filtered to take out the water and we put it all back into our systems. This is really like a closed loop system so we don't have to carryover much water at all. We also regenerate our oxygen system as well. Have a good rest sir, we will be cruising for a while until we get to the Neptune. Very good captain I'll see you then, I also have work to do.

ON THE BRIDGE OF
THE EXCALIBUR

CAPTAIN WE'RE APPROACHING the Calla Neptune, thank you Nav. Com put the Neptune on the wall and holographic image. Aye Sir coming up now. The Calla Neptune was a gaseous cloud at the edge of the solar system. Its amorphous setting ranged in color form pink, to green to a pale blue. It seemed to move within itself changing shape almost at will. At the same time, it seemed to be expanding and contracting in a pulse wave type of harmony. Everyone watching it seemed in awe of its colors and movements.

The captain announced the arrival to everyone onboard, since almost no one had seen anything like this before. Ah, Ambassador you're here, I was just going to have someone come get you so you could see this for yourself. Thank you Captain I wanted to see this phenomenon myself. What exactly am I looking at? That's a good question sir I wish I had an answer for you. This just exists. It's baffled our scientists for a long time ever since it was discovered by a space probe many solsecs ago. It defies our science people. It seems to be made up of dust particles left over from the beginnings of the galaxy. It has held constant in position for as long as we've studied it. It moves within itself, but never leaves its parameters. It stays steady in one position relative to all the rest of the stars. We use it as a way point in all of our navigations throughout this part of the galaxy. Captain it almost seems alive, but I know it isn't. I know I could sit and watch it for a long time trying to figure it out. Why does it change color and is there a pattern to its changes? No on all parts it seems to be random and being here at the fringe of the frontier there are no outside influences on it. It has no gravity of its own, but it maintains position and we don't know why. It truly is an anomaly and I don't know of any others like it. Sir were starting to move into the frontier. Thank you, Nav., Master Engineer are we ready to enter the frontier. Aye sir all systems are go and operating within parameters. Very good let's keep moving. Nav-do you have a good fix? Aye sir all locked in. Sensors go to full scan wide area sweeps. Looking forward there was nothing but blackness. Total darkness no stars, nothing to see. Sir this is like heading into an abyss with no beginning and no end. Yes, it is first officer, cut the visual forward off. People will start to get spatial disorientation. Aye sir video off. Tactical bring up gods eye view on the holographic image. Aye air on. Plot put our heading over layed on the holographic image. Aye sir. A red line appeared with a ling sweeping arc displayed. A small icon of the three ships appeared traversing the red line. There we go people that's about all you will be able to see for a while.

All movement and time seemed to disappear, the only reference point was the holographic image. Time seemed to stand still as one shift folded into another with the only constant being the interior lights and the slight hum of the ship.

Captain this is the Chief engineer. Go ahead this is the first officer the Captain is on his rest period. Well sir, you might want to get him up we have a problem. What's the issue, sir we're slowing down? The main engine is not functioning properly. How so? Its as I suspected the gravity out here is dropping fast. There is nothing out here that we can use to propel us. We know there's no gravity because there's no star systems, but momentum should carry us through. That's the problem sir, I don't know why it happening but it is. Very well I'll get the Captain. Captain to the Bridge please.

Okay first officer what's the problem. Were slowing down sir. The master Engineer says the magneto dynamic drive is going down. How's the cold fusion reactor doing. Fine sir, it's the lack of gravity out here, and for some reason momentum is dropping. That's impossible there's nothing out here to disrupt our momentum. Once in motion and object tends to stay in motion unless there is an equal and opposite force acting against us. Correct sir, but were still slowing down. Master Engineer any new ideas on our problem. No sir I'm baffled, I've rechecked all of our systems and there functioning properly with in parameters. Ok Chief, stay with it. Aye sir. Master chief have you ever seen anything like this before. No sir, but I've never been here before. If we were anyplace else, I'd say we have hit a solar wind wave from a neutron star. But were out here where nothing exists, except us. Core-this is the captain what do you make of our sudden decrease in velocity? Sir I've been working on this issue since I detected a slow don and I've yet to come up with a reason. All systems are working normally and with-in their guide lines. Captain-yes ambassador is there a problem? Well sir we have an anomaly, were slowing down and there is no good reason for it. Sir we've dropped below light speed, what do you want me to do. Master Engineer start the pulse ion engines up and bring them on line if we go below.7 light speed. Aye sir we'll be there shortly. Core this is the captain compartmentalize your search and continue with your normal functions. Aye sir. Captain why did you tell the core to do that. Ambassador the core will chew on this problem and keep adding resources until it can't do anything else. Artificial Intelligence like the core loves these kinds of problems. It's a challenge for them and they get so wound up they lose all efficiency for other functions. That's the way they work, they can't stand not have a solution to a problem. Are we in danger captain? No sir I don't think so, but it is baffling I'll make a note of it in our log for the scientists to work on when we get back. Everyone will continue on as usual, it will just take us a little longer to make our sweep.

Moving further into the frontier the battle group kept their scans going with nothing to report. Just a lot of emptiness with the work cycles coming and going with nothing new happening.

Captain this is Comm, yes, go ahead. Sir I'm beginning to pick up some strange sounds. I can't decipher them, just intermittent sounds. Can you locate their source? Negative sir. They are just coming and going. Put them on the speaker and let's have a listen. Aye sir, here's one now. A very faint pinging sound came through then stopped, a short time later it reoccurred. Sir what do you make of it. I don't know, but it's not just space noise, its definitely machine made. Sir I think its ahead of sus maybe to the port by 10 degrees. Okay let's come to port 10 degrees helm and see what happens. Core-this is the captain define audio transmissions coming from our bow. Aya Captain-it's not much, but I believe it's a mechanical transmission. I'll continue to monitor this phenomena and report back when I have a high degree of certainty as to its origin and relative distance and heading. Very good continue on this heading for a while.

Captain this is the core. Yes, what do you have for us. I have a 50% probability of a distress signal. It's not one in my file, but it could be very old and of low power. Is there a point of origin? No sir there is nothing out here according to our scans. Very good we'll continue on this heading for a little bit further or until you can determine what were hearing. Core could this be an echo from along time ago? No sir I don't believe so its to continuous. If it was an echo then it would just repeat a couple of times and then die out. Very good keep working on it. First Officer what do you think? Sir, its strange way out here I think we should continue by galactic law any emergency signal or transmission would need to be investigated. I agree we'll keep going. Comm any refinement on our heading? No sir it's getting a little stronger, but nothing definitive. Very good let's keep going.

YELLOW ALERT, YELLOW ALERT. The lights dimmed and a yellow light started flashing. Core What's going on why the yellow alert. Sir I've determined the beacon were tracking is an emergency locator beacon of Asantians origin. Its an older beacon but still viable. How can that be there's nothing out here? Sir were getting all kinds of requests form all decks and divisions, if this was a mistake or a drill. Very good open a channel. Aye Sir. This is the captain speaking the yellow alert is not a drill. We have been tracking an unknown beacon signal for a while now. The core has identified as one of our own. We will stay at yellow alert until we determine what and or who it is. Master engineer is this all the speed we can get. Aye sir maxed out at .6 light speed. Very well keep on top of it. Sensors are we at max sensor power Ye sir it's at the widest field available. Very good narrow the field down keep the power high. First officer notifies the Fang and the MaryAnne to keep their sensors on high, but intermittent and change frequencies in a random order. Aye sir.

Captain this is sensors, sir I'm picking up a faint contact 5 degrees port bow. Very good any definition to it. No sir. Stay on it. First officer anything around us at all no matter how small or insignificant. No sir just a lot of nothingness. Captain, I'm getting a better definition, something big not moving. Keep at it. Plot bring up the holographic imaging. Aye sir, but there's not much there, just a little bit of fog or something. Bring it up anyway. If anybody has any suggestions bring them up now. I need input.

Sir we've got more info now. Core what do you make of the sounds and imaging were detecting. Captain-not enough data to support any conclusions yet, but it's strange that both solid mass and electronic signals are emitting form the same relative area that doesn't have anything in it. Core is there something there or not? Answer please. Captain there is something there of undetermined origin. I will endeavor to make better calculations. Captain- I believe you have hurt the cores feeling. First Officer has the artificial intelligence come that far so it has feelings. Not exactly sir but then it is a sensitive being, which its not yet, but I think we're getting close.

Master Chief what's your take on this? Sir I think we've been feed a lot of crap about nothing out here. I think we are on a fool's errand. Somebody knows exactly what's going on here, but there unwilling or unable to tell us.

Duly noted Master Chief, but what do you think we've got here. I think we have some sort of body, planet maybe or artificial even, but I'd be very careful about just charging in due to a distress call. Good council Master chief, first officer goes to red alert. Aye Sir RED ALERT, RED ALERT. The flashing light went from yellow to red. Weapons officer start spooling up all weapons. First officer goes to battle stations. Aye sir. All crew this is the Frist officer man your battle stations, Medical staff go to condition red.

Sir all crew reporting battle station ready the Fang and the MaryAnne are moving into battle configuration 1. Very good nice job. Sir they all want to know what's going on. Sensors what have you got? Sir it's a planet alright, I think it doesn't measure up to what were used to calling a plant, but its there. Very good full sweep lets figure out what we've got. Coming up on the imager now sir.

The Captain moved is chair into the space nearer the image. Very fuzzy can we get better definition and clarity. Negative sir was still too far away, but its some very strange reading. How so? The outlines aren't clear the readings don't match what we normally see. Atmospheric conditions blocking the sensor frequencies. Negative sir, as we get closer it should clear up. Helm slow us up a bit. Aye sir slowing to .5 light speed.

Sir were getting better definition and you're not going to believe this. What have you got? Sir it's not one planet, but two, maybe three very closely packed together. There very small planets, not even dwarf size by definition. How can ha be? Are they in orbit? Yes, I believe so they haven't moved away from each other that's why we aren't getting good readings. They seem to be straight up also not inclined like most planets, very slow rotational speed. By all the laws of physics and planetary behavior they shouldn't exist, but here they are. Any atmosphere? I can't tell to far away, if there is any its probably very small. Core- what do you make of this?

I've been monitoring your conversations and I agree. These miniature plants shouldn't exist. The only thing that is possible is that with no gravitational influences out there the normal laws of planetary physics are either bent or don't work. Either way what we are seeing does exist and they are not man made. I agree thank you for your council and by the way I was not angry with you or your computational skills. Thank you Captain I've always admired your ability to admit your mistakes. Everyone around smiled and raised an eyebrow.

Comm have you isolated the emergency signal yet. Yes, sir why is it coming from all three planets, as they rotate the signal goes out of range relative to where we are. That's why there were intermittent. Who's are they, I don't know yet were going through the registry now we'll have it soon enough. Captain were within visual range now I think there very small and its dark out here. Put it up on the screens.

First officer are the Fang and Maryanne getting this? Yes, sir there all piped in. Well folks this is what all the excitement is about. Your thoughts please. Sir we need to explore this phenomenon. I agree, but I want to know who and/or what we're dealing with. These signals came from one of our emergency locator beacons, but we haven't been out here or any of our ships, much less all three planets.

Sir this is Comm- go ahead I think I have figured out this problem. Go ahead what's your thoughts. Sir I believe we've found the missing Terra Forma guild team. How did they get way out here? I don't know, but those emergency locator beacons probably came from excess military equipment. I've heard they buy some of our stuff cheap so they can outfit their expeditions. Sir I think your comms has got it right, one of my Marine officers did a liaison tour with some Terra Formers before he got is commission and he said they did it all the time. Thank you commander Volarian. The image of the planet cluster had come into focus on the imager. Amazing is all Captain Tallor could say. What's holding them together? Sensors have you got a star on the image, no sir there doesn't seem to be one in the classical sense. There has to be to hold them in position and allow them to rotate in an orbit of some kind. Sir look out at the visual. Is that a blue halo around them of some kind? Sir-could that hold them together? No, I don't think so!

Core is there a star in between the small planets? No sir not that I'm aware of, but there is an object at the middle of the planets, very small not much radiation, but it does give off a blue light, so I think that's what's holding the mini-planets in place. Can you calculate the gravitational forces exerted on the planets? Yes, I've calculated their mass at 4 trillion metric tons. Each planet is roughly the same size and made up of the same material. Generally speaking, silicon, nitrogen, oxygen, carbon and hydrogen. Very similar to our planet make up. I have also detected a very small limited atmosphere on each one. They have artificial atmospheric machines working as we speak. Helm plan for a standard orbit slow to the orbital speed necessary to keep us in the same relative position. Aye sir, but there's not enough room for a standard orbit. Very well set up an orbit that will take us around all three planets as if they were one planet. Fang this is the captain, aye sir I want you on the opposite side of us during the orbit. Mary Anne, Aye sir- plan for a trans polar orbit so that all three of us have the entire quadrant covered with a sensor scan. Sensors-Aye sir split your scan half on the planets and half outward Aye Sir. Core-have you got the orbit calculated yet. Aye sir standard orbit of all three ships laid in and ready to go. Very well all ships slow to orbital speed as the core has calculated. Sensors where's the life signs? Sir there are no life signs coming from planet one and two, planet three is just coming into range. Doctor to the bridge, ASAP. Master chief-what do you make of this? Sir not enough data to make a good observation. But if I was a betting man, there is either no one down there or were to late and everyone is dead.

Sir-we have visual on the planets. Put them up and give me a tactical image of where everyone stands. Aye sir tactical coming up. The image showed three small planetoids in a tight configuration around a light blue shine in-between them. Sensors give me the configuration of the blue halo and center object. Aye sir coming up now with limited data. It showed a methane light coming from a very small shinny object. Sir we've calculated the chemistry of the blue glow. It's definitely methane, with some other trace elements carbon, and nitrogen. Nothing yet on the shiny object. Sir for the log what do we call this thing. Sensors you make the call you found it. Aye sir we'll call it Tri-Par. Very well sensors make the entry in the log.

Doctor I'm glad you could make it. What do you think? Sir its very strange to me. Did the Terra Formers make this, or was it here and they adopted it? We don't know, the problem is there's no life signs. Could they still be down there alive? I've checked the atmosphere, minimal at best. Breathable for a short time, but not for a long term stay. Captain could they have gone underground? I suppose they could, but why would they? Sensors to Captain-go ahead. Sir I've found three small habitats, one on each planet. It looks like they used their transport craft to build habitats for themselves. Maybe there in there waiting for rescue. Comms anything on any hailing frequencies. Negative sir I've been trying ever since we came into range on a broad spectrum of frequencies. Sir the Fang and the MaryAnne report in orbit and holding position relative to us. Very good hold you orbit. Let's get to the conference room and discuss our options.

CONFERENCE ROOM
ABOARD THE EXCALIBUR

OKAY EVERYONE ON, aye sir as the holographic imager came on with the officers aboard the Fang and Maryanne. Well, I'm open to suggestions what's the opinion of all of this. Commander Volarian, sir, this is all very strange, this whole place is strange, but we need to investigate further and try to find out what happened to the Terra Formers. Commander Risig- I agree sir, I think we should send down a landing party and do a thorough search of all three planets one by one. Master Chief- Sir with all due respect if we go to a landing party, we should hit each planet simultaneously and only search within reason of the area around the settlements. I think something bad has happened here and we need to be on full alert. Doctor what do you think? I don't know, but I don't like the idea of no life signs. I would be very concerned about a viral or biological agent they could have been disturbed by the Terra Formers landing on these planets without any information about where these planets came form. Sir are we sure these are planets in the strictest definition. Could hey be a life form of some type that we have never encountered before? Good question anybody want to make a guess? Sensors have you gotten anything that would disqualify these objects as anything but small planetoids or dwarf planets? Negative sir. I can say with relative certainty these were lifeless rocks in space before the Terra Formers arrived. They could have small bacterial remnants in the rocks themselves, but nothing That I would qualify as living. Ambassador your thoughts. Captain I am not a scientist or explorer as you are, but I would be very careful If I were you. This has all the trappings of a Fergie operation and possible trap. We have gotten some good council from everyone, so here's what we're going to do.

Major Pike I want three strike teams of no more than ten Marines per team. Master Chief you will pilot our shuttle craft to the Fang. Commander Risig I want your shuttle to rendezvous with the Fang also. I want each shuttle to take a team of Marines to the surface of each planet. Land close to the settlements and explore the surrounding areas. Full environmental suits and light arms only. Any sign of trouble or hostilities protect yourself and then return to the shuttles. All orbiting ships come to full combat alert any signs of trouble take it out and don't wait for my orders. All teams will come back to the Excalibur were the doctor will decontaminate everyone and everything including the shuttle craft. I want information Major not bodies is that understood. Yes sir-typical recon mission no problem. Everyone stays in touch with each other. I want all shuttles to land at preciously the same time. No laggards. Any questions? Just silence. Very good let's get to it. Master Chief take care of yourself and report directly to me. Stay in close touch with other team members. Aye sir. Doctor prepare the shuttle for full decontamination. Aye sir. Sensors-I want a complete and detailed look at the planet s surfaces. Give me as much resolution as possible. Put it up on the imager, so everyone can see the same thing at the same time. Aye sir. Major Pike-have you selected your teams. Yes, sir squads one, two and three will go to the planets. The remaining squads will be ready incase of an emergency or rescue is needed. Very good as soon as the shuttles get there load up and progress to the surfaces. Aye sir. Doctor to the Captain. Go ahead doc. Sir were all set to go, very well. Chief engineer we'll need the pressurization curtain at full power. The shuttles will be landing one after the other so I don't want any problems we'll have medical personnel in the hanger bay as the shuttles return. Aye sir.

Captain-what is a pressurization curtain. Ambassador it's a translucent plasma curtain that is generated so we can have the shuttle bay doors open and still have environmental and gravity integrity at the same time. The curtain is activated prior to opening the bay doors and shuttles can move in and out without a rapid depressurization. The plasma seals with the shuttles as they move through the curtain. Its not meant to be used all the time, but it can hold pressurization and gravity for a short time. I see thank you.

ON THE SURFACE OF
THE TRIPAR PLANETS

ALL THREE SHUTTLES land at the same time near the small habitats used by the Terra Formers, Shuttle one piloted by Master Chief lands smoothly and with little dirt kick up on the soft green moss like vegetation. Squad one led by Corporal PC disembarks. All six squad members are outfitted in tight fitting environmental suits with helmets made of clear aluminum also tight fitting to here heads. A light cream-colored light illuminates their grim faces. Light hand-held disruptor weapons are carried by each man. There small backpacks contain their oxygen supply and communications equipment. Around their waist is a belt containing combat knives extra pouches of energy packs for their weapons. They spread out in a delta formation moving slowly and deliberately. Master Chief to Captain- go ahead Master Chief. The first squad is on the surface and moving slowly to the habitat. No sign of the Terra Formers or any one else. Very good stay in touch. Corporal PC to Master

Chief-go ahead Corporal. Chief we've got something here. What is it? Sir I've got a body of sorts, or pieces of one. Looks like an arm that's been severed clean as a whistle Now some more, we've got a whole body scattered around my guys are indicating more pieces. Keep moving corporal were taking note and compiling pictures. Aye sir. Captain and Doctor, are you getting this imagery? Yes, Master Chief, Doctor what do you think? I think we have a massacre on our hands. Corporal do you see any footprints or anything that would indicate who might have done this. No not yet we'll keep looking. Captain were entering the habitats themselves we've go maybe five bodies, kind of hard to tell with parts all over the place.

Major Pike what have you got? Captain about the same thing I've monitored your comms and all squads report the same, bits and pieces of bodies. One man has picked up a Sa like the ones we were shown in the Admirals office. Doesn't look like anyone survived. Major what are the bodies, male, female or children. I would say they were all males, no females or children. No sign of a struggle or defense of any kind. All were unarmed, which is standard for Terra Formers. They are pacifists and they don't like conflict. Very good continue searching Major.

Corporal PC to Master Chief-go ahead corporal, sir was in the habitat and in the comm room do you want us to turn off the distress signal. Corporal this is the Captain. NO leave the signal on. In fact, all squads leave the signals on and do not disrupt anything I don't want our presence known.

Captain-this is Major Pike-go ahead, sir we've picked up several footprints and some landing craft marks. The imager showed several rectangular depressions with three bars like deeper lines the Major put his combat knife next to the depressions to give some dimensional features to the image. He then moved over and stood next to a depression much deeper that was shaped in a crescent moon. As he panned out, they could see several more in the distance. In the shape of a triangle. A pretty good size ship I would say heavy and wide. Very good Major looks good thank you and assemble your teams I think we have a good idea what happened here.

Sir, my men would like to bury the bodies, I guess that is the custom of Terra Formers. They dig a hole and put the bodies in it. I guess they believe that they came form the ground so that's where they belong back in it. Strange, but that's their custom. Negative, Major I don't want any sign left that we were here. Sir I think we owe them that, major we owe them the justice they deserve and catch the ones that did this to them. Please return your men to the shuttles and return to the Excalibur. Aye sir will do.

SHUTTLE BAY ON
THE EXCALIBUR

DOCTOR ARE YOU in the shuttle bay with your team? Aye captain were ready for them to return. Very good they should be arriving soon. Captain any idea what they encountered. No doctor, but we will review the imagery of the bodies when everyone gets cleaned up. Aye sir. Captain-this is sensors shuttle from the Fang is on the approach to the shuttle bay with the shuttle from the Maryanne number two to land and the Excalibur shuttle will come in third. Very good get them onboard ASAP and close the bay doors when there all in. Aye sir. Doctor the Fang shuttle is on approach. Aye sir I can see their lights with the other two following. Very good keep me informed if you find any anomalies. Will do sir.

High intensity blue lights shine on the shuttles as they approach to kill all known bacteria and viruses before they enter the bay. The Fang shuttle settles in and the crew members disembark single file through a portable tunnel showering them with a blue light then a chemical disinfectant. They then move into a separate chamber with an antiradiation red and pulsing gold light and finally a high-powered fan. Once they leave the tunnel, they flow into a changing room to get purified clothing and into the bay itself.

Next to land was the MaryAnne shuttle and the process is repeated for that crew. The last to land was the Excalibur shuttle following the same procedure.

Captain this is landing operations the final shuttle has landed and the doors are closing. Very good thank you for the update. Doctor this is the captain how's everyone doing. Very good captain no problems all crew are accounted for and in good health we'll be winding up the decontamination process shortly. Very good I want an officer's call in my conference room when their ready very god sir I'll notify all of them. Sir what about the Master Chief. He's well aware that he joins in all officer's call doctor but thank you for being so observant.

CAPTAINS
CONFERENCE ROOM

ALL OF THE officer's flow into the conference room in their new coverall uniforms that smelled lightly of disinfectant. Everyone took a seat with the Captain at the end. The imager was on with a god's eye view of all three planets and the orbiting craft and their relative positioning.

Okay let's start with Major Pike please report your findings. Yes sir. We found roughly twenty Terra Formers, all males and ranging in age mature males and adolescent males. I would not determine age or name. There bodies were in various stages of decomposition but I think all were killed within the last several solsecs. Method of death was from slicing weapons none seem to have been killed with a laser or disintegrator type of weapon. Various images were shown form individual close in optical readers. All three compounds were ransacked and it appears that equipment was stolen and smaller portions of the terra forming excavators themselves. The larger pieces of equipment are still operating along with the environmental equipment is running normally. The local reactors to power everything is still running. That's about it sir. Doctor your comments please. Sir looking at the imagery I would say they were attacked by a group of assailants that were strong fast and absolutely vicious. Some the wounds were not killing wounds at first, but then they were dispatched later. I have a concern that no females or children were found. Its reported that there were around twelve to fourteen women and seven or so children with this group, where are they? Everyone looked at each other and shrugged. Could they have hidden on the planets somewhere? I doubt it Sensors replied. There would be some life signs even if they went underground. Captain I might shed some light on this. Go ahead ambassador anything would help. Sir I think hey were taken by the Ferugie. No one has said there name yet, but this seems to fit their pattern of operation. I'm afraid they were taken to be sold at a slave auction. We have had similar incidents and have never found any of our kidnapped people no matter what race or origin they were. Just then Master Chief stood up and placed on the table a Sa. I found this near a body and it was stuck in the ground under some moss. I was obviously thrown and either missed or ricocheted off of something. I think this is pretty conclusive proof who the perpetrators are. The Ferugie. The ones were looking for. I think your right Master Chief, but where did they go. There was no ship within the vicinity of Tripar when we arrived. Sir we must find these guys and kill them. Major I know how you feel, but we will take things in order. First where did they go, how many of them are there and once we find them how do we get the women and children back unharmed?

First, we find them any suggestions? Sensors-Captain I might have something, but its pretty thin. I've picked up minute particles of collaboridum. Master Chief and the Captain looked at each other and raised an eyebrow. Go ahead sensors, sir its small but its there. Its from a pulse ion motor that is in poor condition. The first officer speaks up, what's so important about that, it can't mean very much since this place is so strange it might occur naturally. The Master Chief speaks up, sir this element is not natural it's made only by an engine that is either already deteriorated and broken down or is about too. The Master Chief is right he and I have encountered this before on a previous mission, so its real and worth looking into. Sensors set your screen to pick up this element and mark where you find it. We will then move out a little bit in orbit and see if we can pick it up again. We'll make that position and move out again so we'll see after three orbits what we have. It will take us that long to get everyone back to there ship and prepare to leave orbit. Anyone have anything else? Everyone was quiet. Very well let's get going. Plot take us out 300KM in orbit and repeat another 330KM on the third orbit. Aye sir. Helm when you get word from plot take us to it. Aye sir its coming in now. Very good let's do this. Everyone left the conference room. Master Chief picked up the Sa from the table and put it in his sash. Operations to captain, sir the shuttle from the Fang and the MaryAnne are ready to leave. Very well open the doors, when they leave close up again, Aye Sir.

ABOARD THE FANG A SHORT TIME LATER.

MAJOR PIKE ON the bridge of the Fang. Well major how did the debriefing go? Well sir pretty good but the Captain has this hair brained idea about looking for some rare element that his sensors found in orbit. Commander is this guy really that good. It seems like he follows some strange feelings he has and not based on fact. Major the captain is the best we have. He has been on missions that would make the average person crazy His intuitions are the best, just read his record and look at his commendations. Yes sir, but he looks funny with that round misshapen head and his five fingers gives me the creeps. He's so different from the rest of us. Yes, he is Major, but he has the best intentions of any senior officer I have every seen. He thinks about his people first and always puts them at the top of his priority list. You can't get a better Captain especially on a mission like this. We're out here where we've never been before, experiencing things that have never come up before. That's why he was chosen to lead this mission. Why wouldn't he let us bury those Terra Formers, I'll tell you it didn't set well with my men. He had his reasons I'm sure but he's the best we have, so trust him, he won't steer you wrong. Aye sir.

ABOARD THE MARYANNE
ON THE BRIDGE

COMMANDER OUR SHUTTLE has just landed. Very well continue the orbit have the shuttle pilot report to the bridge. Aye Sir. Commander you wanted to see me. Yes lieutenant. How did the debriefing go? Pretty well sir, it looks like the Ferugie are the culprits and were tying to find some rare element that the sensors found in orbit. Really what was it? Collaboridum sir. Never heard of it but I don't think Major Pike is to happy he just wants to kill Ferugie. Well lieutenant that's a Marine for you. We have to find them first and then figure out a way to get to them before they kill the women and children. I know. Lieutenant what was that element again. Collaboridum. First officer have you ever heard of that stuff before? No sir, but I've read a report somewhere about it Give me a minute I'll have core look it up. Very well. Captain this is the core. Go ahead. Your reference to collaboridum, yes. It's a rare element only made by a pulse ion engine that has either broken up or is about to. Any other reference. Yes ma'am, reference to log entry made by Commander Tallor 5 in his mission to the blue planet, now called earth. He found this element had been used by his ancestors on earth 6 generations ago. He found and recovered a knife make with it. It is currently in a museum on our past generations and there exploits to the far reaches of the galaxy. That's about it. You've got to be kidding me. No Commander I don't kid anyone, it must be a vague reference to some collaboridum. No core no further response needed. Commander what do you think? I think he might be on to something; pulse ion engines are about the only thing that works out here and they are very popular with other species to propel their ships.

ON THE BRIDGE OF
THE EXCALIBUR

SIR THREE ORBITS are up. Sensors- tell me you have good news. I do sir on the imager. These show our orbits and the red dots show the element targets. Here's the line connecting the dots. Sir I believe that's their course.

Sensors how sure are you of this plot? Very sure sire I've calculate the chances of this being random and it's not Chances are very high this is where they're going. Very good. This is the Captain we've got a course, break orbit at your best time to form up with me. Plot lay in the course, helm come to new course when you have it. Very good sir we're all set to go. Let's do it, the Fang and the Maryanne have broken orbit and are coming up in delta formation. Very good. Sensors its up to you now, yes sir I've got a good track on the element. I want long range scans in all quadrants. I don't want anyone sneaking up on us. Yes sir, everyone replied.

The delta shaped formation of three ships played through the deep inky blackness of the frontier. Not much was said, everyone hoped the Captain was right in his gut feeling as to the course and location of the pirate ship. Sensors have you got any changes? Aye sir the particles are getting closed together and more numerous. Sir I think we're getting closer. Very good stay with its Master Engineer can we get any more speed out of the pulse ion engines? Negative sir we're at our max now. Very good thank you. All ships keep a sharp look out I think we're getting closer.

ON THE BRIDGE OF
THE EXCALIBUR

SENSORS-TO THE CAPTAIN. I've got them. What's your report Sensors. Sir long range target massive ship on our heading. All ships change to in line formation tight and slightly below each other. Fang move into number two position, MaryAnne move to number three position. Sensors all on passive I don't want to give our position away. Chief engineer gets the cold fusion reactor up to speed ASAP change to stealth mode on the skin. Fang and Maryanne were going into stealth mode so keep a weather eye on us so we don't collide. Sensors any indication they have picked us up. Negative sir I think were still to far away if they have a normal sensor sensitivity. Very good. Plot-take us down a bit I want to come up from below on them Aye air. Down Z2.0 hold steady on X 35.23 and Y132.5. That should do it sir. Very good maintain speed until we get in close then slow to their speed. Aye sir.

ON THE BRIDGE
OF THE PAAG

CAPTAIN THE MEN are getting restless, food supplies are down and they haven't had any meat in a long time. So, first Officer what do you want me to do about it. They'll have to get along until we get home. Sir we didn't bring aboard enough supplies at our last refurbishment stop. Because you said we couldn't afford it. You said that we would pick up food stuffs on the next raid. Those stupid little Terra Formers don't eat like we do and had little supplies just these stupid pills. Again, first officer I can't change that I didn't know they wouldn't have any supplies. Sir the men think that you intentionally didn't buy enough food so you could pocket the ration money. First officer your beginning to bore me with your insolence and bordering on mutinous deeds and actions. Sir I'm just repeating what the men are saying. What do you suggest you insulant welp? Sir, why don't we let them have one of the female hostages to eat. That will shut them up until we get home. Very well then take one of the older women, just be reminded that her value in the slave market will come out of there shares. That's not right sir, well that's the way it is I'm the Captain and that's my decision.

Captain-yes sensors. I'm getting some strange readings here. What are you seeing? Sir I thought there were some targets behind us. Then they disappeared, then again it was like a shadow there. Check your equipment sensors, there's no one out here but us. Aye sir. Captain, check out complete nothing there and the equipment is working fine. Very good. Engineering can we go any faster? Negative sir the port engine is just hanging on as it is, I can't push it any harder. I told you before we left that we needed an overhaul, but no you said we couldn't afford it. INSOLANCE that's all I get is INSOLANCE. Back in the day no captain would tolerate it, you all would have been quartered and eaten. When we get back, I'm going to replace the lot of you with men that don't complain all the time and are happy to be working and sharing in the bounty that I create.

ON THE BRIDGE OF
THE EXCALIBUR

S IR WE'VE GOTTEN about a close as I think we should be. Very good helm slow us down and match their speed. Sensors have you got a full passive scan? Yes, sir coming up on the imager. A large T shaped ship appeared. The main fuselage was a large circular tube attached to a smaller circular tube forming a T. The stern was cut back at an angle creating a ramp that folded upwards. Several large pods were in position along both sides of the fuselage. A large narrow hump ran from the forward section down a third of the fuselage. What do you make of her? Sir it looks like a large Corallin transport but with additions of the humps and blisters along the side. Very good I agree Commanders anyone seen anything like this before? Negative sir, but we agree it was probably Corrilian at one time. The large engine pods in the stern are the give a way. I agree. Master Chief your thoughts please. Captain the large long pod on the dorsal looks familiar. You saw that too. Yes sir. If I remember correctly there was a certain Cribari transport that had the same kind of addition. I always wondered where it came from. Gentlemen this is commander Risig would you like to fill us in on your thoughts. Yes, sorry commander, Master Chief and I ran into a Cribari transport a while back he had the same kind of addition. It turned out to be a secret laser type weapon that transports are forbidden to carry. We almost ran into a trap. Suckering us in close with our shields down. Luckily my ensign weapons officer recognized it in time and fired. Unfortunately, the ship exploded because it was carrying a very heavy load of Methane crystilate that was being stolen and resold. Yes sir, I heard of that incident. We have to be very wary with this crew and ship.

Sensors can you penetrate the hull with our beams without being detected. Yes, sir I just have to be very slow so they don't pick it up. Sir I think this ship is more sophisticated than it appears. There sensors screens are very up to date and very precise. I'm surprised they haven't pick us up yet. Maybe they have, but just not showing it. I don't believe so sir no alarms or alerts going off. How many life forms are they carrying? About forty on the main deck in the port and starboard crew areas. There is a room in the maid hold area with maybe fourteen to sixteen there. They are all huddled up together. Sir I'd say there the hostages. Life support is minimal so there lucky there small. Any openings on the fuselage or is it all on the upper deck. No openings per se, but them seems to be a small man type door next to the ramp in the stern. How much pressurization in the main fuselage? Minimal if any the sealed room is the only pressure vessel other than the main deck.

Major Pike are you on the bridge of the Fang? Yes, sir I'm here. Do you have a small contingent of Marines that could do a solo deep space transfer?

Yes, sir my marines are trained for it. Good, then get them ready I'm calling a red alert for all crafts. The red lights began blinking on all three ships. Sir what's the plan?

First, I want a squad or less of Marines to leave the Fang and do a deep space transfer to the Ferugie Vessel. They should go to the stern and find the man door by the ramp.

Second, I want the Maryanne to slowly move up directly under the Ferugie and hold station until I order it to move forward quickly in front of the Ferugie ship. Staying in front and let them see you. Order them to halt and be bordered. I doubt they will comply, but I want you to create a distraction enough the keep their attention away from the exposed Marines.

Third I want all shuttles to form up with the Fang and pick up the full contingent of Marines. And be ready to move to the Ferugie vessel.

Fourth I want the transfer marines to blow the door when the Maryanne starts firing. Once inside they lower the ramp door. It looks like the controller is right next to the man door. Once the marines are inside, they move directly to the confinement room, blow the door and grab the hostages. They should take with them enough environmental rescue bags to put each Terra Former in the bag. I assume all pressurization will be gone by then. they will have to be fast, they wont last long with the limited environment leaking out.

Fifth I want the shuttles to move forward and dock inside he main fuselage. There should be enough room discharge your marines and capture of kill any and all Fergie's. If possible, I would like to capture the captain and officers alive. But not at the parrel of the marines. The hostages should be loaded onto the Maryanne shuttle and returned to the Excalibur. I will move the Excalibur to the Starboard side facing the Ferugie out of stealth mode. I would like the Maryanne to take up position opposite me on the port side. The Fang will move up and back up near the lowered ramp to provide any assistance to the other two shuttles and marines as needed.

Well Major how is that for a plan? Sir it sounds great how did you do that so fast? Situational awareness Major. Commanders any questions?

Captain how do you want me to proceed after I fire first on the Ferugie. That commander is up to you. You do what seems right. I will warn you thought that the first shot should be at the weapons control station after that is up to you. Very good sir, thank you for the opportunity. I'm not doing you any favors commander; these guys are born killers they will hold no quarter for a female and they might have a lot more fire power than we anticipate. I understand sir. If there are no more questions then let's get to it.

Master Chief be careful out there and keep an eye on these young Marines I don't know how many of them have actually been in combat before. Aye sir I don't think there will be any problems.

ON THE OPEN STERN RAMP OF THE FANG

SIX MARINES STOOD on the ramp looking out at the abyss that was the frontier. There tight flat back environmental suits blended with the darkness. Their packs full and everyone tethered together. Their helmets were dully lite outlining their faces, each had a small rifle type of weapon and a strapped down side arm. Fighting knives strapped to their lower left leg. Corpora PC have you ever done this before. Yes, number three once. There's nothing to worry about. Corporal PC had a bullet shaped device in is left hand and room for his right had to hold the other side. Just relax the thruster pod will take us directly where we need to go. Corporal PC are you and your team ready came through on there helmet communicators. Yes, sir just give the word. The bay light silhouetted the six Marines against the darkness. Then go go, go. They released their magnetic boots and yelled UGHRAH as they leapt into the darkness.

ON HE BRIDGE OF
THE EXCALIBUR

COMMANDER RISIG MOVE out ordered the Captain. Be careful the marines breaching team is out there. Just then the MaryAnne moved under the Fang and under the Excalibur then quartering in under the Paag. She moved slowly directly under the belly of the giant ship and stopped just aft of the cross member. Captain how do you stand the pressure asked the Ambassador who was standing near the captain. It's the training and the full confidence of the team we have assembled. Sensors how are we doing?

No indications we've been spotted sir. I just hope the breaching team gets there fast I have a feeling this game is about to blow up. I agree. Doctor assemble your team in the shuttle bay and prepare for causalities. Aye sir were on our way.

BREACHING TEAM
IN THE ABYSS

CORPORAL THIS IS six how are we doing? Hang in there six, corporal I'm getting dizzy. Ok look up and to your starboard I can see the Paag. Oh, there it is. Stare at it for a while, you'll be okay. The corporal was following a projected green image on the inside of his face shield. It showed a red line and the coordinates of their position and distance to go to the door. The image showed the large ramp and man door in the stern of the ship. We're almost there everyone start pulling up on your tethers starting with six. Shortly everyone was together hanging on to the foot of the man ahead of him. Then CLANG as the propulsor struck the heavy metal door they were aiming at. Their outside helmet lights came on and showed the door and the opening mechanism and locking pad. Corporal PC clipped his tether on to the handle securing the team to the PAAG. Number 2 pull up and place the charge on the door. Aye corporal as he pulled himself up and retrieved the small magnetic charge and placed it on the opening mechanism and door pad. The team then pulled themselves around the corner of the ship and activated their magnetic belt vests each had on his middle pack. Everyone around the corner aye came the voices behind him.

Captain this is corporal PC, we secured to the PAAG and ready to blow the door. Very good came the voice in his helmet standby. When the action starts blow the door, but not before Aye Captain.

ON THE BRIDGE OF
THE MARYANNE

COMMANDER RISIG BEGIN your run and good luck the breaching team is secured to the Paag, but be careful when you get to the stern incase, they have a problem. Aye sir we'll watch for them but tell them to keep their heads down the Paag is about to face hell.

With that the MaryAnne moved forward as fast as they could in front of the Paag did a fast-outside Immelmann and was facing the Paag in a blur. They put the MaryAnne in reverse to hold position relative to the Paag.

With a booming voice on all hailing frequencies Commander Risig challenged the Paag.

ON THE BRIDGE
OF THE PAAG

W HAT THE HELL, said the first officer as they looked out of the windows of the bridge. Here was an alien frigate class ship directly in front of them.

Commanders Risig female voice boomed over their communications system. "This is the frigate MaryAnne and we demand that you heave too and prepare to be boarded. If you do not, we will be forced to shut you down and board at our discretion.

This is the captain of the transport ship Paag. You have no rights here in the frontier and you will not board my ship. If you do it will be an act of piracy and we will have the right to defend ourselves. I will not be boarded by a female much less than a real boarding party. The voice then said we have a warrant from the galactic court that authorizes to board and detain anyone that is considered to have broken the general laws of the galaxy. Captain I order you to stand down and be boarded. If everything is in order then you will be allowed to go on your way.

ON THE BRIDGE OF THE EXCALIBUR AND MARYANNE

S IR THEY'RE POWERING up their weapons. Commander Risig noticed a slight movement on the upper level of the fuselage. Her orders were instant and strong. Weapons lock on to their weapons command and control systems. Aye sir ready to fire. Commander this is the captain fire when ready. Aye sir firing.

The first shot was a golden ray of energy emitting from the upper level of the fuselage. It tore through the front glass window and into the weapons control station on the port side of the bridge. It exploded immediately as the oxygen in the atmosphere turned into plasma. The next shot came almost instantly into the control room next to the weapons station. The three crew members were immediately charred to a coal like mass. The explosive depressurization of the bridge sucked all three crew members out before the automatic shut downs activated that prevented the rest of the crew from being sucked out. The Paag crew activated the red alert system as they came to battle stations.

The captain commanded the breaching team to blow the door. Almost instantly corporal PC hit the charge button. The charge exploded immediately with a dull thud and the door blew open and the environmental inside pressure banged the door outward. Debris and dirt billowed out into space. It was over in an instant and the team scrambled in as fast as they could. Corporal PC found the ramp opening levers and pulled them all down. The ramp began to move slowly as air rushed out pulling a large amount of dirt and small debris items into the vacuum of space.

ON THE BRIDGE
OF THE PAAG

T HE STUNNING ATTACK temporarily disoriented the bridge crew as the captain bellowed out orders. Red alert, red alert all crew members prepare to repel boarders. Sir the operations crewman said he hull has been breached, I know you idiot I can see the hole in the bridge screen. No sir, no sir the rear ramp door is opening and the man door next to it has been blown open. Viewer on the hold looking back. the image came up and he could see the ramp coming down. Stop the ramp. Sir the control has been either overridden or destroyed there is nothing we can do up here. The captain could see the crew members scrambling out onto the upper cat walk the surrounding the cavernous hold. Sensors how the hell could these people get so close without being seen. Sir I don't' know, but if you remember I thought I saw something and you said it was nothing. The Captain pulled out his Sa and flung it at the insulant crew member, striking hm in the head and killing him instantly.

ON THE BRIDGE OF
THE MARYANNE

As soon as the MaryAnne fired she moved upwards did an inverted roll. This put her upside down relative to the Paag. Commander Risig ordered all weapons system to fire independently as targets came to bear relative to her slow forward movement. The first to feel the fire was on the large rail gun that was just beginning to appear out of its well. The gold colored disruptor ray melted the gun from the muzzle to the breach It never made it out of the well completely. Simultaneously the port and starboard mini disruptors fired at the blisters along both sides of the hull. Their golden rays immediately blew apart the blisters and everything that was inside of them The Paag was leaving a large trail of debris behind her. All disrupters were firing at anything that looked like any kind of weapon system. Nothing ever fired back Unaware to her the initial attack on the weapons control system knocked out all control of all weapons systems. A fatal design flaw of the designers.

As they came to the stern all fire was directed to the engine pods on each side of the fuselage. The port engine that was just barely working took one hit and it exploded immediately and was ripped from the hull it went into space falling apart and the pieces tumbled irradicably. The port engine stopped working as soon as it was hit. The constant fire though shredded the pod and the inside working pieces hung loosely off of the hull but stay attached. Commander Risig ordered cease fire as the inverted MaryAnne went over the last edge of the stern. She ordered an outside loop that put them on top of the Paag and out of the way of the shuttles that were starting to move in. Commander Risig moved the Maryanne to the port side and pivoted her around so she faced the Paag opposite the Excalibur.

BREACHING TEAM
INSIDE THE PAAG

ORPORAL PC AND his team moved slowly and quietly along the port side wall heading towards the front of the ship. There lights were off so they blended into the dark inside of the ship. They could hear a terrible racket outside as the MaryAnne kept firing into the ship. The explosions inside were made louder as the echoes rang out. They moved forward and soon the saw movement on the upper catwalk. Corporal this is three there all over the upper catwalk. I know they haven't seen us yet so keep moving. Just then bright lights shown in form the outside as the shuttles moved in with there landing lights on full. Just then a Sa came flying overheard. They heard The SWISH as it just missed number three. He instinctively Fired his weapon. A bright green ray came out and caught the offending Ferugie in the center of his body and he dropped to the deck. Corporal PC yelled stop firing and move faster we have to get to the hostages. The rest of the Ferugie didn't know what to do the shuttles were getting closer and ready to land. All of a sudden, a dull rumble was heard and the team was slammed into the wall at their backs. The Ferugie yelled and squealed in pain as the intensity of the wave hit them. Luckily the breach team was behind some equipment when the wave hit. What the HELL was that five and six yelled. I don't know, commented corporal PC but let's get the hell out of here and get to that room. The light was bad, but after a few steps they came to another door. This is it, number two get up here and blow this door. Aye corporal as he edged forward and put another magnetic device onto the locking mechanism. They all pulled back a bit and knelt down. Instantly the door blew in a loud thud and they raced in. In a standard clearing technique, each member went into the room with there hand the man in front of him shoulder and his weapon at the ready in opposite direction. Corporal PC turned his light on and immediately lite up the room, nothing but containers and just then number four yelled out over here. The lights focused on the corner and a huddled mas of small people in rags were cowering on the floor. Their breathing was hard and labored sucking for air. Quick everyone get your bags open and just throw them in one per bag and seal it up. They all went about grabbing the women and stuffing them into the bags. They kept saying breath slowly your going to be okay. One woman holding two kids tried to fend them off, but didn't have the strength. Number six was standing there and opened a bag and the two kids both jumped into the same bag. That's okay seal it up there small the bags can handle them. As soon as the bags were sealed, they blew up using their own self-contained air supply. In a short time, all the hostages were in their bags and they were inflated. Corporal PC said tether at least two bags to each of you. I don't want them to float away and get caught in the fire fight. They all tethered up and moved to the door. Getting ready to come out of the door into the hold they saw the scene of an intense fire fight going on. The shuttles had landed and disgorged their marines and they hit the ground firing up in all directions of the swarming Ferugie on the upper cat walks.

ON ALL THREE
SHUTTLE CRAFTS

FROM THE OUTSIDE of the Paag they could see the MaryAnne as she made her way down the hull of the Paag. Upside down as she was firing all three disruptors at the same time. The golden rays ripping through the armaments of the Paag like slicing through cheese. Everyone just starred with their mouths open at the sight. The MaryAnne was moving slowly to the stern and debris was flying in all directions. The trail of destruction was immense all the ships were moving at the same pace. The MaryAnne pulled up nose high as she made it to the stern and did a 180 degree turn during the outside loop when she came around moving forward and on top of the PAAG. Amidships she turned left and did another pirouette movement to face the Paag. MaryAnne this is Master Chief on the Excalibur shuttle. I have never seen flying and maneuvering of a frigate like that in my life. Well done, well done indeed. Thank you Master Chief I learned it from your boss.

Well its time for us to get to work I hope there something left of the inside. Master Chief this is the Captain there are life signs of Ferugie through out the hold. Major prepare for a warm welcome when you land and be ready to fight the moment you stop. Thanks Captain we will.

The first to land was the Fang shuttle in the middle of the hold the bright landing lights lite up the inside like day light. The Excalibur shuttle landed to the right of the Fang shuttle. The Maryanne shuttle landed to the left by the wall where the hostage room was located. As each shuttle stopped the Marines were on the move, they all moved into covered firing positions by the cargo in the hold. Each man firing upward to the opposite side of the catwalk as they landed. The gold and green lasers and disruptors firing at will. The howling and screams of the Ferugie as they were hit rang through the hold. All of a sudden, the marines felt movement in the floor. Major Pike yelled into his communicator to everyone to activate their magnetic boots. The floor wasn't moving, they were. The artificial gravity on the ship was breaking down and they were beginning to float free. The boots worked and they stayed in position. The Ferugie weren't as lucky. A lot them were fighting without there boots on since the attack was so sudden. They began to float free of there cover positions. This was the end for them the marines took aim and shot them as they came up. In no time the firing ended and the dead Ferugie bodies were floating all over the hull.

THE BREACHING TEAM

ORPORAL PC AND his men left the room in the midst of
the fire fight keeping low and against the wall with the
bags against the wall and their bodies protecting the bags.
Sa's began fling again as the Ferugie saw them. The air by
now was so thin the sa's went in all directions since they had
no air to give them good flight characteristics. They moved
deliberately along the wall to the MaryAnne shuttle. The clam
shell doors opened with the upper door going up and the lower
door moving down providing a stairway. As each marine got
to the door, he shoved his two bags into the shuttle and got
out of the way for the next man. Soon all of the hostages were
safe inside the shuttle. Corporal PC ordered five and six to go
with the shuttle and help the hostages. They both protested
that they wanted to stay and continue the fight. Corporal PC
said no the hostages need you more. Get going. They both
jumped in and the doors closed. Let's get out of the way and
the four men jumped behind some heavy cargo just in time,
the shuttle began to lift off and then backed out. Corporal

PC and his group moved over to the Excalibur shuttle where they encounter Master Chief firing his weapon as he aimed at the Ferugie on the railing. Then a terrible shriek bellowed out as a Ferugie that had worked his way in close jumped up and moved towards the Master Chief with his Sa held high and twirling as he moved forward. The Master Chief stood up and growled showing his teeth as well and moved forward. Just as they were about to meet the Chief fired his weapon at point blank range. The gold stream of the particle disruptor hit the Ferugie in the center of his chest he fell backward and then up as his dead corpse floated away. Just before he got out of reach the Master Chief grabbed upward and took the Sa from his cold dead hand. The Master Chief just looked back at the marines and said well boys that's the way it's done where I come from.

Corporal PC and his group moved forward and to the starboard side of the hull where they found Major Pike. How's it going sir they asked. Major looked back and said what are you guys doing here? Well sir we came up to go with you wherever your going. Were going up there as he pointed to the catwalk stairway. Let's go as he moved forward to the base of the stairway. Major Pike yelled into his communicator give us cover fire. Instantly a barrage of disruptor fire blazed out from all directions. They ran up the stairs as fast as the magnetic boots would allow to a secured doorway.

Do you guys have any breaching charges left? Yes, sir yelled number 2. Blow the door and be ready this is the bridge. As they moved back the charge blew and the door swung open. They moved fast each man entered the room pointing in opposite directions and keeping low.

THE BRIDGE OF THE PAAG

THE BRIDGE WAS Smokey and had low red emergency light s blinking. A massive hole was on the port side where the disruptor beam blasted through and took out the control stations. They could look forward and see nothing but the inky blackness of space. Luckily the hull de-compressors were still working keeping some atmosphere still in the hull. They moved forward careful examining each nook and cranny with their helmet lights blazing. Soon a noise was heard to the far starboard side and they found several Ferugie huddled in a corner. They yelled at them to get their hands up but nobody moved. They motioned with their weapons and still no one moved. Finally, a high-pitched voice yelled out "don't shoot, don't shoot" We won't if you come out with your hands and arms up with no weapons. Soon the mass began to move and one after another the Ferugie moved in their hands and knees. This must be the bridge crew piped one of the marines. Yes, they are said the high voice.

Each marine grabbed a Ferugie and dragged them away. They all had on emergency hoods over their heads that allowed them to breath. The marines picked up the Sa each one had in his belt sash. The last Ferugie knelt up and his teeth began shattering with a menacing look in his eye as it came up from his head on an antenna. It trashed around. Major Pike grabbed the eye as it came to him and he squeezed. The grimace on the face of the Ferugie told him that this was a very sensitive spot for them. Major pike yelled out once their hands are secured grab the eye and hold it real tight. This they did and found the Ferugie became very placid and relaxed. Corporal PC Secure this guy's arms behind him. Aye sir. Major this guy has four arms how do you want him secured. Use two sets of prisoners securing straps behind him and then through the waist sash. Aye sir. As Corporal PC was doing this, he spied the brightly shinned Sa stuffed in his sash. He grabbed it and put it into his belt. The Ferugie squirmed and the major squeezed his eye again and he let out a terrible howl. Why don't we just kill them all and add them to the body count said number two. We can't number two the Captain wants prisoners. This guy just might be what he wants. A slight movement caught everyone eye and a creature appeared that no one had ever seen before.

He was a long worm type of being with small black legs running the length of his body he came out of hiding and soon the front half picked up and stood upright. He was a pale yellow in color with several black spots running down his back. He wore a red and white scarf around his neck although it was hard to distinguish his neck from the rest of his body. He ad on thick goggle type of glasses covering is two black eyes. The lenses made his eyes look bigger than they were. He said in a clear voice, my name is Luscious and I'm a Centalorian. I speak around a thousand languages and I'm at your disposal to help translate for you. Major Pike could hardly get any words about. Finally, he said are you armed? No sir I don't carry weapons and I don't like violence in any form. Good who is this guy. His name in almost untranslatable, but he is he Captain of this ship called the Paag. What are you doing here and why are you with these pirates? Sir I was hitching a ride to Panku Peku. They told me they were traders and I accepted the ride. When they came back with the hostages, I knew they weren't trades. I had no choice but to stay on. Very well come with us. Is your emergency helmet working okay? Yes, sir thank you for asking. Okay Marines lets get ready to move out.

ABOARD THE EXCALIBUR

I**T WAS HECTIC** aboard the Excalibur, the shuttle from the Maryanne arrived with the hostages. Everyone went through decontamination escorted by the medical staff and the marines who came with them. The bay crew helped with the hostages and kids that were scared and trying to get acclimated to their new surroundings. The women were scared with all of what hey had been through. Captain Tallor was busy trying to coordinate the landings and keeping up with the fire fight aboard the Paag. The Master chief and he were in constant communication with how things were going. So far this was a text book operation. The hostages were secure. The ship was a riddled mess but was stopped.

Captain this is Major Pike. Go ahead Major-Sir the Paag is secured. It's a bloody mess though we've got bodies floating all around. We're trying to secure them as best as we can, but I don't have the manpower or equipment. Don't worry about it Major how's your Marines. Very good sir no causalities as far as I can tell at this time. We have several wounded, nothing major, some lacerations and on ankle got turned over. Sir we've got four Ferugie prisoners, one is the Captain. And one strange fellow. What do you mean strange? We sir you're not going to believe this, but he calls himself and Cernturalian. Sir he's a big worm, but he claims he speaks a thousand languages. That is strange Major, get you and your men back ASAP. Aye sir clear the bay were on our way.

The next shuttle to land was the Fang shuttle carrying the Marines. They got out and went directly in decontamination. The Excalibur shuttle waited outside of the bay to let the de-contamination team catch up and clear the way. The Marines got out of the de-cont. tents laughing and telling of there fight with the Ferugie. Their uniforms were trashed and they enjoyed the fresh air and clean one-piece uniforms provided. Then the Excalibur came in and landed with the prisoners and corporal PC and his squad. Major Pike lead them out of the decon- tents. Each marine was dragging a Ferugie prisoner their arms secured behind their backs. The last one out was Corporal PC dragging the Ferugie Captain, who was spitting and choking and coughing. What's wrong with him corporal asked the Captain. Sir he didn't like decon. So, I sort of had to force him through. I think he swallowed to much fluid.

Master Chief how goes it? Very well sir, we kicked their collective ass and gave them a thorough trashing. It's been a while since we've been in a hand to hand combat sir. I thourghly enjoyed it, but I must admit I was a little rusty at first. Well you look no worse for wear and I see you've picked up some extra hard ware, pointing at two Sa's tucked into his belt. Yes, sir I did, pulling one out and handing it to the

Captain. Thought you'd like a little souvenir for your blade collection. Than you Master Chief for thinking of me. Your welcome sir it's a pleasure.

Major Pike walked up saluting sharply and said Sir I present you the Captain of the Paag. Corporal PC dragged the Captain up to where he was standing. A little behind him came the Centalorian. Sire, I would like to introduce my self to you. I'm Luscious he bowed slightly and lowered his head. Luscious I heard you were among the Ferugie, but are not part of the crew. No sire, I hitched a ride with them from an outpost in the Clorian system. They took me to Panku Peku their base. I was looking for work. I couldn't secure a position so the Captain here said he would take me back to the outpost on his next trip. I said I would be happy to translate for him on his trading stops and he said fine. Sire they never went back to the outpost and instead raided up and down the frontier. The last one was the place where they picked up the hostages. I knew sire I was in trouble then and just hoped to get back to Panku Peku in one piece without being eaten. Sire, did you know they were cannibals. Yes, Lucious I heard they were, but never knew anyone actually witnessing that. They are sire I saw it myself.

The captain turned to the Paag captain and asked what his name was? He just stared and a slight grin came to his mouth and he chatted his teeth. Just then the last Ferugie moved and jumped at the Captain with his mouth open, surprising the Marine guard with his speed and agility. I midair Master Chief twirled around and pulling his Sa from his belt he slashed into the air. The Sa caught the Ferugie just above the head, severing his antennae and eye. The Sa continued and cut the tops of the Ferugie pointed ears off. The Ferugie let out a horrible howl and fell to the deck. His severed eye rolled away and stopped. Corporal PC immediately drew the shiny curved Sa from his belt. He simultaneously pulled up on the Captains eye and antennae at the same time. This movement made the Captain howl in pain. The sharp pointed end of the Sa was pushed up under the Captain's jaw, so hard that it drew a small amount of blood. Corporal PC asked "can I kill him now sir it will be a pleasure?" No said Captain Tallor, I want him alive to go to trial and have justice served that way. He doesn't deserve a quick clean death.

Chief Engineer clap these prisoners in irons and strap their mouths shut with cargo tie downs. I don't want them to be a danger to any guards or crew members. Aye sir, I'll have to go back to the Paag and get some heavy metal sir, we don't carry enough on board for the replicators to make the irons. Very good take a survey crew with you and do a thorough inspection to see how sable she is. Aye sir, with your permission I'll have Master Chief transport us over there. Very good, in the mean time lock them into a metal storage container. Aye sir. Master Chief thank you for your quick action you saved me again. Let's get this mess cleaned up and get everyone some rest. Corporal PC and the rest of the guard marines dragged the prisoners to the storage compartment. On the way there he made sure to step on the eye of the Ferugie that made a squishing sound. The Ferugie took notice and stayed compliant.

Lucious tell me again about this Panku Peku. Well sire we were heading for it when you stopped us. It's a small binary system. The two small planetoids orbit around a tiny blue star. Very similar to the system you just came from, but it has two planets instead of three. Are these common in the frontier. Yes sir, they are; some have one planetoid and some have two. Three is an exceptional cluster. I don't know of any that have more than three. Do the Ferugie run this Panku Peku? No sire no one really runs it. They stay pretty much on their planetoid and the other one is the settlement Panku Peku. It's sort of a way station and trading post in that part of the frontier. The main person is a gentleman named Bernado Din. He owns and runs the trading post if you will. His emporium specializes in weapons and imported spirits. Master Chiefs eyes light up and says "spirits" as in drinks and imported ales. Yes, exactly, I don't partake in strong beverages myself, but he certainly has a well provisioned store. The sign outside of his shop says Bernardo Din Weapons dealer and purveyor of fine spirits. Sounds like my kind of place Captain, maybe we should pay him a visit. My thoughts exactly Master Chief. Lucious does this Bernado Din trade with the Ferugie. Yes sire, he trades and services the Ferugie vessels. You see he also runs the space port operations. How many ships do the Ferugie have? Two sire, the Paag and the Columbine. They're both exactly alike. Very good Lucious you go with the doctor and have her take a look at you and rest up. Sire your not going to "clap me irons" like the Ferugie. No Lucious as long as you promise to behave yourself and not get into any trouble. I will sire, you know we can't lie it's against our nature. I don't think I have ever heard of a Centelorian ever lie or tell a miss truth. I know and thank you for your help. We'll talk again.

Master Chief take the engineering team back to the Paag, secure the bodies and see if there's anything we can do to repair the ship. Aye sir. Oh, Master Chief also see if we can get anything out of her computer or core if they have one. Especially the coordinates of this Panku Peku. Will do sir. But honestly, I don't think there's much left. I appreciate anything you can do Chief. Aye sir.

ABOARD THE PAAG

MASTER CHIEF WHY don't you check out the cargo and see how much heavy metal is available. Will Do Chief Engineer. I'll go to the bridge and check out the computer. You men there, start grappling those bodies down and secure them to the deck with magnetic shipping straps. Lieutenant, why don't you set up the Gravaton so we can walk easier it some gravity. Aye Sir.

The master chief starts looking over the cargo and making mental notes on the size and configuration of the cargo. He works his way to the front of the hold. His partible light shining around he spots a tarp that hides a large object. With his curiosity up he peeks under the tarp and shines his light in. Low and behold there's a

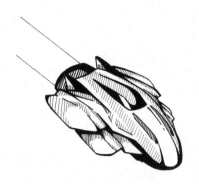

large shinny object there. The light scans the front of it and along the side. It has a pointed nose and some fins or something that travel the length of the body. He pulls more of the cover back and revels a small ship. The likes he has only seen in imagery from his past. He lets out a low whistle and rubs the smooth skin. By now all he can do is pull the tarp completely off and it floats to the upper deck.

The STX is has a short-pointed nose, each side has two sets of fins, one traveling the length of the body and gong upward. The lower fin travels the length of the body and bends down as it travels the full length. The landing gear consists of a forward slid and the aft gear is a skid on each side. The skids retrack into wells at the base of the ship. Small thruster ports are located on the nose cone and the aft portion of the upper and lower fins.

The fins are large enough to provide an air foil effect when traveling though an atmosphere. In the stern of the ship are two large exhaust cones that direct the pulse ion engines. They are also used for exhaust of rocket fuel mixture of Hypergolic peroxide and oxygen. This is the fastest two-person vessel in the galaxy. Under the nose are ports for two disruptor weapons.

Master chief is running his hands along the outside of the vessel which is shinny cold and extremely smooth. About a third of the way back from the nose he feels a button on the underside of the upper fin. When he touches it, he hears an unlocking sound and the side of the body and wings moves upward. He backs out of the way and the door opens all the way up. He can't help it so he crawls in and sits in the pilot's position. By the time he gets settled the door starts to close down. He immediately puts his hand out and the door stops and retracts upwards again. He looks at the controls and the screens in the cockpit. The whole front of the ship is transparent aluminum only visible out and not in. From the outside the hull looks solid metal. He looks up and the switch panel is on the ceiling. He starts flipping the switches and immediately the front panel lights up the landing lights come on the interior lights come on. He orients himself to the panel layout, it's similar to other ships he has piloted. To the lower left are more switches, which are the environmental controls. To his right and slightly back is the co-pilot seat. He notices that the panel in front of the co-pilot is a duplicate panel. This ship was used for pilot training. Behind both seats is a small storage area and ae electronics rack that held all kinds of boxes and wiring. He flipped the switches to the off position and everything shut down. He got out and just looked in awe at this sleek small shuttle craft. He was standing there and the Chief engineer came up. Watch 'a got their old boy? Look said Master Chief. Its an STX he exclaimed, where did it come from? I don't know, but I know where its going. I'm claiming this ship as salvage according to the galactic rules on free trade and abandoned property. 'she's all ours Chief. I just want to see the Captains face when you show up with this. I think he'll be alright with it honestly. I would not put money on it. You know him he's a stickler for following the rules and property. Come on let's get it to the ramp so I can fly it out of here.

The Chief engineer calls some of his men over and they un strap the STX from the deck. They place some lines on it to control it. With the weightlessness the STX begins to rise. The men with their magnetized boots gently pull the small ship around the rest of the cargo until they get it to the back of the Paag and rachet it down to the outer ramp.

Master Chief, we've gotten the survey done and I've got the guts to her computer so I think were ready to go. Very well Chief, I'll fly the STX and you take the shuttle back. The Chief looks a bit dismayed, I haven't flown in a long time, I hope I can remember how. Don't worry Chief I'll set the shuttle on auto-land and it will fly itself. Okay let's go. The chief and his men scramble into the shuttle and slowly back out of the ramp. The Chief calls the Excalibur and tells them he's landing, not waiting for them to reply.

The shuttle approaches and lands gently into the hanger bay of the Excalibur. Master Chief jumps into the STX and flips all the switches on.

The STX gently starts to vibrate as the turbo pump spool up and soon everything is green on the annunciator panel. He pulls gently back on the right control lever and the ship backs up and into free space. He presses the right foot pedal and the ship pivots on its own axis. Both left and right sticks forward and she accelerates slowly but smoothly forward heading back to the Excalibur shuttle bay. Master Chief announces his plan to land and on approach. The shuttle bay controller comes on and says "say again please". Master Chief tells him the STX is ready to land. Laughing could be heard in the background as the controller gives the okay. As he comes in and hovers in the bay all the bay crew members were gapping at the sleek little craft. The controller tells him to put it down on the far-left side of the bay to stay out of the way of everything else. Master Chief sets it down gently and tuns everything off. The door opens and he gets out to an applause from the ground crew. Master Chief could do nothing but smile all the way.

CONFERENCE ROOM
ABOARD THE EXCALIBUR

ALL THE OFFICERS crowd into the conference room. It was unusually crowded because the officers from the MaryAnne and the Fang gathered around the outside of the large conference table. The holographic imager was on showing a god's eye view of the Paag with the, Excalibur off to the starboard side, the Fang slightly behind the Paag and the MaryAnne on the port side. All ships were holding position as the Paag had just about slowed to a stop.

The captain at the head of the table starts out. "First of all I want to congratulate all of you on a mission well done Your professionalism and skills were apparent through out this entire operation. I will be making recommendations to the Admiralty staff for all of you. Major Pike your marines were outstanding. Especially your breaching crew. That was a dangerous mission especially entering a ship with little or no intelligence on their enemy. Well done." "Thank you, sir I will pass along your kind words and recommendations.

One thing we've all been wondering. What was that huge rumbling noise and energy beam that hit the Paag right after the breaching crew entered the ship?" Sensors it was your idea please explain yourself. Well sir I thought we needed an edge when the hull breaching crew entered the Paag. All of the bridge crew was focusing on the MaryAnne and the Ferugie were starting to gather to assault the bay area. So, I hit the Paag with a controlled sweep of the main sensor area. This close in I thought that it might disorient the Ferugie enough to give your men an edge. I think it worked! It did, but it would have ben nice to have some warning. It flattened my men against the wall. Good thing there was a lot of heavy equipment around them to absorb the main force of the energy. I never thought it could be used as a weapon. Nor did I major, but we learn something every day.

Let's go around the table and get everyone's report. Doctor lets start with you. "Very good sir. There were three minor casualties among the Marines, two lacerations and one twisted ankle. All are doing fine, there will be no lasting effect. The Terra Forma women and children are doing pretty good especially with all they've gone through. They are all eating fine and doing well now that they are breathing our atmosphere."

Chief engineer. "Yes sir, the Paag is a mess, no power, no gravity, no atmosphere inside. The hull has too many breaches. Basically, she's dead Commander Risig did a fine job, considering she only had one pass at her. The dead Ferugie are strapped to the main deck as best as we could sir. Some body parts are still floating around but there's nothing I can do about that as long as she's still open to space. The computer is in engineering and some technicians are working on it, but it's so old no one really knows how it works. Captain it's a binary computer. No one has seen one of these things in a life time. We have installed an interface with it and the core, with several buffers in-between. Well see what it can come up with."

Navigation what do you have. "sir as best as I can tell were about in the middle of the frontier. Hold on sir. Sir the core has just gotten back to me.

I'll put it on the imager. Up came several lines and circles through out the frontier. Sir the red line is projected path the Paag was on when we intercepted, he. The yellow line is the path that she took when she left Panku Peku. The yellow circle is a stop at an out post, still working on the name. The line extends to another outpost. As you can see, they are all in the frontier just skirting known solar system. The next yellow circle is Tripar. They might have gotten information on Tri-par at the last outpost. Please note when they left Tri-par they were on a direct line to Panku Peku. A new circle popped up at the end of the red line. Sir that's the location of Panku Peku.

Very good nav. Looks like the core broke the binary code of the computer from the Paag.

Plot-what do have. Sir the imager tells it all we can move towards Panku Peku as soon as you give the word Very good.

Master chief what do you have. "Well sir first of all I would like to congratulate the Marines on a job well done. Next, I would like to take this opportunity to tell Commander Risig and her crew that what I witnessed was some of the best flying and maneuvering I have ever seen Just watching the MaryAnne coming down the length of the Paag inverted and firing at the same time was like the wraith of death hovering over its next subject. Well done indeed. The damage to the Paag is immense Captain she can't be salvaged or towed or anything. Sir she is a hazard to navigation even if it is the frontier, Sir we can't leave her where she is." I agree Master Chief anyone have any suggestions?

Sir I might have an idea! Go ahead sensors. Sir I've noticed a small anomaly to our port side not too far off. I've studied it sir and it looks like a small and I mean very small black hole. Sensors are you sure? How could a black hole be out here? Sir I know, but how could there be a tiny blue star with planetoids circling it. Okay go ahead what's your theory. Sir If we could steer the Paag a little bit to the port side and put her into a tail first position we could stick her into the black hole. That would hold her into a perfect position forever or until it chews it up. That would be a very long time. We could put a non-directional beacon on it that would warn others in the area. We could also register the position with the galactic navigation board making it a waypoint named Paag. Very well thought out Sensors thank you.

Chief Engineer what do you think. Well sir it could be done I think we could put some fuel into the thrusters that are not damaged and steer her that way. The nondirectional beacon is doable and I think we could rig up some permanent nav lights on her. Its doable sir. Very good Chief you've just gotten your next assignment. Go ahead and get started.

Sir-Yes Doctor- what do you plan on doing with the Terra Forma people and the Ferugie captives? Any suggestions Doctor? Not really, but I don't think it would be a good idea to take them all the way to Panku Peku. I agree doctor,

Commander Risig, I would like to have you and the MaryAnne take the Terra Forma people back to Asanti. Please take the Ferugie captives with you and drop them off at the galactic court on Centurri 2. It should be just about on your way. Major Pike please assign two or three marines to accompany and guard the Ferugie. Sir permission to speak freely? Go ahead Commander. Sir I don't think its wise to split your forces. We don't know what's ahead of us on Panku Peku. Sir you might need all the firepower you can get. I don't disagree with you commander. But I also have the responsibility of the civilian Terra Formers to think about. I'll note your concerns in the log. I am going to prepare all of the documentation for the court to consider on the Ferugie and make my recommendation for punishment. Please prepare your ship and crew for departure. Chief Engineer please move the shipping container with the Ferugie in it to the MaryAnne, ASAP. Aye sir.

Chief Engineer please make your preparations on the Paag to move it to the little black hole. Aye sir will start on it immediately. Chief keep me informed on your progress and let me know if you need anything. Aye sir.

Doctor would you please have Lucious come up to see me. Yes, sir is he in trouble? No, No I just want to have a talk with him before he leaves on the MaryAnne. Yes sir.

Master Chief would you join me in my quarters. All eyes went to the Master Chief as they filed out of the conference room. The Chief Engineer came up to Master Chief and whispered in his ear, I think the old man knows. Aye not much gets past him.!

IN THE CAPTAINS QUARTERS

M ASTER CHIEF WOULD you like to explain to me why you brought an alien craft on board my ship with out my permission. Sir it's not like that at all. I found the STX onboard the Paag when we were doing our inspection. I've wanted one ever since I heard they existed. They are the fastest most maneuverable ship in the galaxy. I thought it would be too much of a waste to just let it go. Their so rare and I thought history would never forgive me if I let go and not keep it for posterity sake. I even thought if might be useful at some time. So, I saved her. I made sure it was clean and not contaminated in any way. Have you checked to see who the real owners are? Yes sir, I checked and all of the numbers and symbols have been carefully removed there is no way to find the real owner. I fact sir there was a time when these machines were assembled by individuals with no manufacturing codes. I think that this is what happened to this one. Sir if I may, this machine was claimed as salvage under international galactic code, that states "any object or goods confiscated as an act from pirates, smugglers and persons of ill-repute can be considered in the ownership of such person that makes lawful claim, witnessed by at least two other individuals that can swear to the nature of the claim" That's very good Master Chief you quoted galactic regulations extremely well, as if I didn't know them myself. Thank you, sir, I figured you would want to know the exact quotation for your records. How is it Master Chief that you seem to be able to squirm out of just about any situation that you might find yourself in? Sir I don't squirm, I just like to point out the facts as I see them and hope that the person listening has an open mind, Sir as I know you do.

Knock on the door. Come in calls the captain.

Sir you wanted to see me? As Lucious was standing in the door way. Yes, come in Lucious. Sir I'll beg my leave and let you talk with Lucious. No Master Chief please stay were not done yet. Yes sir. Lucious I wanted to tell you that you will be leaving on the MaryAnne to go back to the galactic court. You will be heard by the court and they will decide what to do with you. Lucious head hangs down and says aye sir in a low muffled tone. Lucious don't feel down about this. I will report that you have been very helpful to us and that you saved my life when the Ferugie tried to attack me in the shuttle by. I'm sure they will take all of that into consideration when they hear your case. I will be very forth right in my explanation and make sure they grant you all considerations. I will also recommend that you be retained by the court as an interpreter for them so you will have gainful employment and be a credit to your family, which I know you want. I think you will be very happy living on Centurri 2. It has a very pleasant atmosphere and a lot of well-educated people that will be a pleasure to be around. Lucious' head comes up and he smiles from his little mouth. He stands straight and slightly shakes at the thought of his good fortune. Thank you Thank you very much sire I will endeavor to make you proud of your decision about me. No problem Lucious. I do have some more questions for you. Go ahead sire I'll do the best I can. I'm sure you will. Lucious how big is Panku Peku. Sir its about the size overall of Tripar. It has two small planets. The main planet where the outpost is has one small village type, that's where Bernado Din has his business and space port the other where the Ferugie has their main base is slightly smaller. The base is really a walled compound. Pretty large made of stone. There are two gates very large and lockable. There are generally two guards at the outer gate. Then you go through a small open area and you get to the Main gate. It also has two guards on it. Once you get through it leads to a main open area in the main building. This building is pretty large with high ceilings and a lot of stuff hanging over the walls and down from the ceilings. This is where the main Fergie's stay. Outside of this compound is a space port when the ships come in and dock and unload their cargo. They refuel and leave for another "trading" mission. Can both ships land at the same time? No sir just one at a time its not that big. You say there's just the two ships. Yes, sir the Paag and the Columbine. Anything else you can think of that will help out. Just one thing sire. When you get close to Panku Peku be careful there's guard buoys out there that let them know if any ship enters without there permission. Are they armed? I don't know sire. I think there's some kind of code to get through. I'm not knowledgeable about such things. Thank you, Lucius you have been very helpful. You can go and get ready to leave. Yes sire, will I see you again? Probably not Lucius the Master Chief and I don't get to the galactic court very often. It seems the Master Chief is not a welcome person in those parts. It seems he had an incident a long time ago. I think it had to do with one of the judge's wives. Master Chief just looks to the ceiling and grumbles something. Lucius just miles and says thank you again for all you have done for me and I'll take my leave. Lucius bows deeply and walks out. A lot of good information sir. Yes, we'll have to come up with a good plan on this one. I want to avoid a big fight if at all possible. Master Chief, think about this and get back to me I'll do the same. Very good sir do you want me to inform Commander Volarian and Major Pike? No not yet I want to think abut this a little bit. I know what Major Pike will do, a big frontal assault with a lot of fire power.

I don't want a lot of civilians getting hurt and a lot of collateral damage. Nobody knows were here yet and I would like to keep it that way. Aye sir

ON BOARD THE PAAG

THE CHIEF ENGINEER and his team start the task of activating the Pag's thrusters and outfitting the ones that were damaged with small auxiliary thrusters from the Excalibur. On the bridge they wire in a remote-control unit that will fire the thrusters. They also place small imagining units outside on the hull facing aft. One close to the stern and one on each part and starboard side of the bridge. The imager on the belly was original to the Paag and they reconfigured it to the Excalibur's controller unit. This will give them a completed view all the way around the exterior of the Paag. The inside of the Paag was left alone except for the gathering of more heavy metal incase they need more to replicate into more restraining chains for future captives. The work went fast and soon they were back aboard the Excalibur.

ON THE BRIDGE OF
THE EXCALIBUR

CAPTAIN THE CHIEF engineer and his team are back aboard. Very good ops have the Chief Engineer report to the bridge Aye sir? Master Chief what do you think? Sir I think this will be a very tricky maneuver. The Paag is a giant ship and the amount of thruster activation will be pretty good. The mass of the ship is huge and once you get it going in one direction it will tend to stay on that course. It will be delicate and take a deft hand on the controller unit. Very good Master Chief said the Chief Engineer as he walked up to him and handed him a small hand-held controller. Don't look at me Chief Engineer you're the one that rigged that contraption up not me your responsible for its outcome. The Captain just looked at both of them and grinned.

Gentlemen, I'll fly the Paag and take full responsibility. They just looked at him and both said Captain no disrespect, but you haven't flown a toy much less a giant of that nature. The Master Chief grabbed the controller and asked the

Captain for his chair. Very well Master Chief it's all yours. Master Chief settled into the Captain's chair and moved to the center of the Holographic imager. Master Chief in a commanding voice says: I've got the con." Plot give me full imager on the Paag and stay with it all the way. Aye Master Chief. Helm as the Paag turns to the Port stay above it and just behind. Fang please move out the way. Aye responds the Fang, Maryanne please move out of the way I want a clear view of the Black hole. Aye comes the response. Plot keep giving me heading updates in X, Y and Z positioning. Aye Master Chief. Master Chief activates the small controller and the lights come on all green. Gentlemen were all green prepare to move. The right stick controls the port and starboard thrusters. The left stick controls the pitch up and down thrusters. Both sticks forward propel the thrusters forward and back activates the breaking thrusters. The thrusters start firing and shortly the Paag begins to move. First, she pivots tail first until she's facing the Excalibur. She then goes slightly downward on the stern. Plot calls out the coordinates. Navigation calls out position to the black hole and rate of speed to the black hole. All four ships are now moving in unison as the Paag slowly picks up speed. The entire bridge is quiet as command flow and coordinates are called out. Nav-are you sure of the position of the black hole. Aye sir your heading straight for it closing slowly. I can't see it. This is the damnd'st thing I've ever done, flying a giant ship backwards into a balck hole with out even seeing it. It's their Master Chief it's just very small. Then imperceptibly the Paag starts picking up speed Fang and Maryanne do you see anything? Master Chief I can see a small ripple or something in the darkness Came back the Maryanne. All ships turn on your landing lights full brightness. Almost instantly the darkness lite up. Master Chief this is Plot- the Paag is picking up speed on its own I think it's caught the gravitational pull of the black hole. I suggest you only use port and starboard thrusters to guide it in. Sensors-how do we look on the Y coordinates to the hole. I don't want to go over or under it. Your fine Master Chief You might want to slow it down a little the mass of the ship might be too much for the hole to take if it runs into it too fast. Thank you. Master Chief starts the braking thrusters a little at a time.

Master Chief to all ships start pulling back now. Helm go to all stop and let's see what happens. Aye Master Chief. Soon little by little the Paag pulls away from the Excalibur. The outside cameras now show the black hole getting bigger and bigger as the Paag moves closer. Master Chief pushes the stern of the Paag down with the thrusters mounted on the tail and raises the nose of the Paag up. This aligns the Paag with the orientation of the black hole as the Paag settles into its final approach to the black hole. Then as the cameras on the stern look directly down into the black hole they go blank. From the outside, the massive ships bow suddenly tilts upward. The ship stops moving except for a few vibrations and the then stops all together.

Everyone on the bridge claps and stands up at their posts and Yells MASTER CHIEF, MASTERCHIEF. Master Chief turns and moves over to the Captain. Sir the Paag has landed and will be forever known as Waypoint Paag. Outstanding Master Chief I knew you could do it. Master Chief hands the controller to Chief Engineer and says "nothing to it, just like primary flight training" Chief Engineer claps him on the back and says 'well done indeed

Couldn't have done it better myself". I think we could all use a drink from the Master Chief's private stock. Aye I'll stand all of you to a pint at the Boar and Dragon when we get home.

Sir the directional beacon has activated and as you can see the navigational lights are on. Very well everyone nicely done and congratulations. Chief Engineer what did you use for a power source for the controls and beacons. Sir I used some extra bi-lithium crystals from the cold fusion reactor. They'll last a lot longer than all of your 7 lifetimes put together. Very well thought out and executed. Captain this is navigator I'll notify galactic Navigation and Space control of the coordinates and the name Waypoint Paag. Very well nav.

SHUTTLE BAY THE EXCALIBUR

Everyone gathers in the bay the shuttle for the MaryAnne has its doors open. The terra former women and children gather around and start boarding the shuttle. Commander Risig and the shuttle pilot stand next to the Captain. Captain I wish you would reconsider this move to send us back. commander I have and I think this is the best curse of action for the women and children. Here is the package of court materials you'll need when you get to Centurri 2. Chief Engineer has moved the container with the Ferugie in it to your ship. They are well shackled and confined. You have two Marines that will stand guard on your journey back. Under no circumstances are you or any of your crew to open the container. These are dangerous criminals and I don't want anyone to get hurt. I understand Captain I will carry out your orders to the letter. Very good then get on your way. You have all of the coordinates and navigational data necessary so good luck and fair winds

Commander. She smiles and waves good bye. At the stairway she says, Captain if you haven't noticed there are no winds in the frontier. The door closes and the shuttle lifts off.

The doctor comes up and says "sir do you really think it's a good idea to send them off with the Ferugie on board, what happens if they get free? The Captain smiles and says" I pity the Ferugie if they do. That lady is as tough as any marine or man I've ever meet. They would do well to give her a wide berth. Okay let's get back to business.

IN THE CAPTAINS
CONFERENCE ROOM

ALRIGHT, LET'S GET back to work. Plot-do you have the course the Paag was on when we stopped her? Aye sir. Sensors put up the god's eye view of our current position and over lay the course projection for the Paag. The imagery pops up and the Captain moves over next to the image. This then should be the course to Panku Peku. Navigation have you gotten the course laid in? Aye sir. Helm bring us to the projected course and the coordinates to Panku Peku. Very well then let's talk about what we do when we get there. Suggestions anyone? Commander Volarian-sir I think we should do a complete scan of the binary planets, announce to the Ferugie that they should surrender and take them prisoner. Major Pike- Sir I agree with the commander, up and until we order them to surrender. Sir they will not surrender especially on their home planet. We saw how viciously they fought defending their ship. I can only imagine what it would be like on their planet.

We would have to do a full-scale attack on the plant first and then send in my marines to mop up what's left. I fear we would still take a large amount of causalities. We don't know if they have civilians there so I fear there would be a lot colleterial damage to them. Doctor-any comment. Sir we've been lucky so far in not taking any causalities. I would suggest scanning the planet and try to determine what were facing down their first. If there a lot of them, then just blockade the planet and call for major reinforcements before we take any action. There're could be thousands of them down there and we would be out gunned and out manned. I think it could be a disaster. Chief Engineer-sir I'm not a strategist or military planner, but I think the doctors plan deserves a lot of consideration. We are lacking a great deal of information. Let's do a complete scan first. I agree Chief Engineer, but a complete scan would give them notice we are here and provide them with time to organize their forces and plan an attack on us. All the heads nodded in agreement. Master Chief-Sir I think we should approach very carefully and keep our presence hidden. We don't know their level of sensor sophistication. We should study them carefully. Then I think we should send in a scouting party of no more than two or three people in disguises to serval the planets and see what were up against. Just a short visit so as not to arouse suspicion. Report back here and discuss and make a plan. Sir what's your idea. Master Chief We've been together too long, I like your idea, but would take it a little further. I think we should do a recon mission ourselves. Everyone up here will watch and have all of the ship's armament focused on the Ferugie planet. The other planet where this Bernardo Din lives will be off limits for attack unless we find that the Ferugie are there also. Our little friend Lucious said that the Ferugie stay pretty much to themselves and only trade with this Bernardo Din character. Once we get the lay of the land and determine what forces the Ferugie have then we can determine what type of attack we should use. First Officer- sir I don't think you should be in this recon mission. You're to valuable if something goes wrong. Sir I would like to take your place. Thank you, First Officer, but I will need you on board. You know this hip better than I do and we would need you to look after things if all hell breaks loose. Major Pike I would like you to have your marines at full alert. If we run into trouble, we'll need you to pull us out fast. Yes, sir we'll be ready for anything, but you must understand Captain we will do whatever needs to be done and we won't worry about collateral damage Sir. Very well Major you've just named your own poison. Helm how long until we get there? Not to long sir, it's really pretty close. Sensors passive scan full ahead, look for some guard buoys. Lucious said they were out there and we needed a pass word to get through. Aye sir. Go to full stealth mode, Commander Volarian bring the Fang up in close just like we did with the Paag. That seemed to work pretty well I think our stealth devices work a little bit close into the ship, at least Aye sir.

The battle group picks up speed and heads directly for Panku Peku the Fang tucks in close to the Excalibur. All running lights are off and the sensor wave in front, though not visible reaches out into the darkness

PANKU PEKU

SENSORS TO CAPTAIN, sire were very close, Helm slow down let's creep in Aye sir. Sensors any sign of the guard buoys? No sir not yet. Did Lucious say how far out they were? No. Put up visual. The walls came alive with the darkness and then a faint blue halo started to appear. There it is sir. Yes, I see it sensors anything yet? Yes, sir just showed up One to our starboard close in and one further out on the port side. All stop lets hold position here if we can. Aye sir we'll drift a little in, our momentum will carry us through the arc made by the buoys. Full reverse on the thrusters, I don't want to break any beam between the buoys.

Passive sensor scan of the planets. Aye sir. What do you think Master Chief? Sir there pretty ominous looking just two black balls in space with a blue halo around them. Sensors what do you have. Well sir first images coming in now. Put them up on the imaginer. Gods eye view please with our relative position. Aye sir coming in now getting better detail the more we stay here sir. Very good. The imaginer showed two small planets the one on the right was slightly higher in orbit than the one on the left. It showed a rough terrain with a large building and a space part landing pad next to it. The one on the left showed a small settlement with numerous buildings and a space port leading pad just a short distance away. The buoys showed as bright yellow spots with several blinking spots in orbit around the plants. Sensors-why are there blinking yellow lights? Sir sensors picking up intermittent returns, so they are blinking. I would assume those are part of a constellation of buoys around this place. I don't think they want anyone sneaking up on them. We would have blown right through them if we weren't for warned. Yes, it's pretty much as described by Lucious. Lets held here for a while and see if we can get any more detail. Is there any signals traffic from the planet? Not yet sir, were scanning all of the known frequencies. Very good continue your scan. Any sign they know were here? Not yet sir. I don't think they have any deep space sensor activity at all.

Master Chief what type of disguise would you recommend? Sir I'm all prepared I have what we'll need down in the shuttle bay. Very good Sensors is there any good place to land a shuttle down there so we won't be seen. Scanning sir but I don't think so. As soon as you break the barrier between the boys, they'll know your coming. Crap says the Captain. Sir if you will indulge me, Yes Master Chief go ahead. I suggest we use the STX

It will go well with our mercenaries cover story of being here to look for the Ferugie so we can get some work. It works well for us being here in a small ship and we should be able to ask questions of this Bernardo Din and get some help meeting the Ferugie. Our disguises will provide an extra layer of authenticity. And sir not to be to forward we will need to hid your round head and five fingers. Everyone just looked around with their mouths open. I understand completely Master Chief I like that idea. I just hope we can pull it off. First officer- Captain I agree with the Master Chief. This is a trading post of sort with traders and travelers coming and going all the time in your disguises you will hardly be noticed. The more I hear the better I like it. Sensors how are we looking at the smaller planet. Very good sir, we've got good resolution now. Not much there. A few buildings with several larger than the others, I think they look like warehouses. The space port is decent size so the STX should be of no problem. A short walk from the space port is a large building that sits at the end of the main road. Terrain is relatively flat pretty plain all the way through. The other planet is a different story. Made up of mostly rock pretty heavy stuff. The main structure is surrounded by a large wall also made of rock. Looks like a main gate through the wall then another smaller wall with a gate and then the main structure. Comprised mainly of rock with some ceiling material I can't identify yet. Inside I've got a lot of life forms they seem to match the same configuration as the Ferugie captives we had. The numbers are inconclusive but a lot of them maybe a hundred or so. Very good sensors, how about the other planet with the village? Maybe a hundred, but no Ferugie all different types of life forms, looks like a sampling of the entire galaxy. Good so then our disguises should fit right in. Aye sir it should unless someone recognizes you? I don't think so sensors, since none of us has been in the frontier before. Master Chef let's get down there and see what we can see. First Officer you've got the command keep a weather eye out for problems. If we run into a situation, we can't handle have Major Pike and his marines come running. Aye sir, keep your communicators close. Will do.

IN THE SHUTTLE BAY

THE MASTER CHIEF was already in the bay when Captain Tallor arrived. Both were in civilian clothing consisting of almost knee-high leather boots dark trousers one black and the other dark brown. Master Chief wore a light blue pull over tunic that came to just below his waist with a bright red sash tied around him with his highly polished Sa attached. The sash had small metal fibers woven in that were magnetized which held the Sa firmly in place. He wore a dark blue over coat that had long sleeves that hid his hands. Unbuttoned. On his head was a large black floppy hat with a wide brim that fell loosely down almost covering his face. The Captain came walking over to him. Master Chief where did you get that outfit? I've had it for a while now it has served me well in the past on other covert missions. Here's yours Captain Tallor wore high dark brown leather boots. His trousers were black and he had on a pale-yellow tunic that fell below his waist by a substantial amount He had a brown sash around his waist, which also had a light

115

magnetized metal strands running through it. No Sa but a large knife off to his left side that was also magnetized to stay in place. Master Chief handed him a large black over coat with long sleeves that hid his hands. Master Chief threw him a large floppy hat similar to his except his hat had a tall pointed portion that disguised his round head. It also had a wide brim that partially hid his face. The captain put on the coat and hat and they both got into the STX. The doors closed and the panel lite up as the switches were activated. The engines started with a light whim as they came up to speed Master Chief looked at the Captain and said let's go if your ready. I'm ready came his reply. Two restraining bars that were U-shaped came down and pushed them lightly, but firmly into their seats. The STX lifted off and backed out of the bay. On the radio came good hunting from the controller of the shuttle bay.

IN THE ABYSS

THE CAPTAIN BECAME fully aware of the inky blackness the surrounded him. He said "this is the closest I've gotten to the loneliness of the frontier" Aye sir it is that. You've really got to give it to those Marines on the breaching team to have gone through this with only their environmental suits on. I'm sure glad we have men that have that kind of courage. They need to have their commendations upgraded. Here we are in a ship and they had nothing unbelievable. I've never felt like this before Master Chief. This is really disorienting with no stars, no horizon or anything. Sir were coming up to the buoys. What's your plan Master Chief? Just blow right by them with out giving them any notice and hope that don't shoot first and ask questions later. Good plan.

Just past the boundary layer they could see the blue halo and the planets in front of them. The speakers in their helmets came to life. Violating craft, you have entered a restricted zone do not come any nearer. This is the SYX craft, sorry for violating your space, but we are short of fuel and need to land immediately. We are here to see Bernardo Din Can you help us? There was a slight pause and then the reply. Proceed straight ahead and land on pad number 3 It will be designated by the flashing light. They were moving pretty fast and shortly they saw some faint lights. As they approached closer the light began to flash at regular intervals. They flew a standard left-hand approach and lightly touched down on a big number 3. Say in your craft came the order until someone comes to get you. Yes sir. Master Chief shut down the engines and opened the doors. The restraining bars lifted up and out of the way. Master Chief and Captain took off their helmets and put their floppy hats on. Shortly a small artificial intelligence rolling vehicle came out and shined a bright light in their faces. Both men reacted by putting their hands in front of their faces and yelled to get the damned light out of their eyes, since they were so sensitive. The light dimmed and the artificial voice said excuse me I didn't realize your species was that sensitive to light. Well we are snarled Master Chief, take us to Bernardo Din. Yes, sire came back the little robot. They got out of the craft with their hats on and started to walk down the roadway to the large building in front of them. It was several stories high with a large front door. Over the Door in several languages was BERNARDO DIN WEAPONS DEALER, TRADER AND PURVEYOR OF FINE SPIRITS. They climbed the two steps and walked in. The shop had a wide variety of weapons stored on racks on both walls. There was a transparent showcase with well over 100 small hand weapons. The further down you went the larger the weapons. They could see in the back wall was a large barreled weapon of unknown origin, but it looked ominous.

A man appeared and walked toward the Captain and Master Chief. He was slightly taller than the Captain well built. He had on a pair of fine medium brown leather boots, dark brown trousers, a pale-yellow silk tunic with a green sash. His head was round and hairless. He had on a dark brown open vest that came past his waist but not quit to his knees. His head had a soft cloth covering dark brown to match his vest. A very finely adorned person of obvious wealth and status. Around his neck was a black box that hung down to the middle of his chest. His eyes were emerald green and his skin was smooth and a dark cream color.

Hi, my name is Bernardo Din and I'm the owner of this establishment, what can I do for you. His voice came from the box around his neck. It was a universal translator. He was holding up his right hand with the palm facing them. Were looking to find work and were told to see you the Captain exclaimed. Bernardo looked at them both taking in what he saw. It is customary in this part of the galaxy to introduce yourself when meeting a stranger, so with whom am I addressing. Sorry claimed the captain, I'm five and this is Chief. Bernardo looked puzzled and said you both go only by one name? Yes, the Chief said, we don't want to seem rude, but we've been out of polite society for a while now and we need to get used to it again. Any name is as good as another in our line of work, I see said Bernardo what type of work are you looking for and how did you get my name? The Captain said "we are looking for security work and we ran across a little fellow at a trading post in the Clorian system. His name was Luscious and he was a Centalorian.

He was hitching a ride with a Ferugie trader. He mentioned your name so we thought we'd come to see if you could help us. Yes, I think I remember a Centalorian like that. You don't see too many of them especially out here.

A small man walked up. He was wearing a green tunic and green pants. His feet were covered in ankle high boots with the elongated toes rolled up. He was diminutive and had flaming red hair on his head as well as his face. He wore a gold chain around his neck with a gold pendent shaped like small four bladed leaf This, gentlemen is my assistant Shamus. Everyone held up their hand except the captain he kept his hands folded across his chest with the sleeves covering them. Bernardo Din we would like your men to get our ship refueled and looked after. He smiled and said excellent he pulled up his sleeve a little bit and talked into a small wrist held box. A moment later he said his men will look after the ship, refuel it and make any necessary repairs. He said it was unarmed, we could reload it for you if you wanted. Chief said very good because we dodn't want to be traveling around unloaded, we heard there were pirates in the neighborhood. Bernardo laughed and said you have to be very careful here in he frontier, there's bad folks all over. The captain was looking around and said you have quit supply of armament, yes Bernardo Din replied I do have everything from complete shipboard systems to hand held personal protection Bernardo came over to the chief and lightly touched his coat and pulled it back He saw the Sa attached to his sash. That's quite impressive Chief how did you come by the Sa? Master chief said I took it from a dead Ferugie. He tried to kill me with it, but obviously didn't succeed. Bernardo looked at him and said Yes indeed. Five what are you looking for I see you don't have a Sa. No, I just carry this and he pulled back his coat and revealed a large knife handle encrusted with silver and a dark ebony handle. Bernardo moved back to the counter and said look around I'll be happy to show you gentlemen whatever you like. Master Chief said where do you keep the fine spirits? Ah, Shamus will show you. This way said Shamus as they walked down to the back of the shop.

The Captain was looking around and on the front wall about half way up he spotted a weapon that was covered in dust. Bernardo saw him looking at the weapon and went over and pulled it down. He put a piece of fine leather on the transparent show case and laid the weapon on the leather. He wiped off the dust and presented the weapon to the Captain. What is it? This my friend is a rare weapon I took in trade from a Cribari merchant man.

I don't know where he got it, but its interesting. Like nothing I've ever seen before. It has a hammer that pulls back, the cylinder rotates one notch. He called this curved bar a trigger that activates the hammer. The hammer falls and strikes a cartridge that fits into the cylinder. This then fires a projectile out of the barrel. The hand handle was curved and rounded at the bottom. This weapon fires six times then you have to reload it through the little door that opens up. Sounds pretty complicated to me. Yes, but it sure makes a lot of noise and smoke. The projectile is large and makes a very big hole at whatever you're shooting at. Why did the Cribari trade it? He couldn't shoot it other than with two hands. It's a very clumsy design. The Captain looked closely at it and saw the engraving on it. What does it say? I don't know it's a strange language that's not in our data banks. How much do you want for it? Bernardo responded, five gold credits, I'll even throw in the two boxes of projectiles and a carrying sling. Well that sounds awfully expensive It's not really for such a rare piece. The Captain picked up the gun with his hands out of the sleeves. Bernardo stepped hack and said OH MY! The Captain held it in one hand and pulled the trigger back and squeezed it. The hammer fell and he pulled it again several times over and the gun reacted the same way. He held it in both hands and tried firing it with either hand. Bernardo was stunned at what he saw. Looks pretty good to me. You see it was designed for a person with five fingers like me and not for three like you and the rest of you people. The Captain laid the gun down and said how much again, five credits came back Bernardo. Well I'll give you one half a gold credit for it and the ammunition and the carrying sling. Oh no Said Bernardo I couldn't part with it for that, I've gotten to much into it. The Captain said well how many five fingered customers have you had in here lately that could shoot it. Well none really said Bernardo. I'll tell you what I'll give you one gold credit for it right now take it or leave it. Bernardo smiled and said you've got a deal. They both held there hands out in front of them with there palms facing each other.

The Master Chief came up and said Five you wouldn't believe the stock Bernardo Din has. He's got at least five different kinds of solarian ale it all taste delicious. He then noticed the Captains hands were out of his sleeves and Bernardo was looking closely and smiled at them both.

No how do we get in touch with the Ferugie? Bernardo looked quizzical and said I can arrange to have you taken over to the Ferugie base. The leaders name is Peritas, but he likes to be called Emperor. Where did they come from? I don't know Bernardo said. They just showed up here a while back. They settled on Beta. They've been here ever since. They came in a very odd-looking ship. Then shortly afterwards the Columbine landed. They have been trading ever since. They then came in with the Paag. So, I assumed they traded their ship for the two of them. I service and sell them fuel and provide a place for them to trade out their goods that they bring back. The only thing I don't deal with is the people. I don't like slavery and won't tolerate them bringing them here. Where do they go with them? I don't really know, but I've heard the they have a slave market on a small outpost in the Thorian system. Shamus what's the name of that place? I can't recall sire, but it's the only one with two suns in the entire system.

Where do you two hail from? Oh, just around we don't stay in one place very long just to get the job done and then we move on. Bernardo Din what made you settle here? Nothing in particular, just got tiered of the same old political stuff that happens in all the star systems. Out here we don't have to deal with it. What bothers you the most about the politics of the star systems? Well take for instance the Laurincians They were a pariah on there neighbors and the only thing that happens to them is they lose their ability to travel outside of their own system. I've heard a rumor that they have teamed up with another star system to do their bidding. Oh, which one is that? I don't know, but I think it's the Asantians. Why them? Because they have the ability and the desire to expand their empire. What better way than, to up and be able to blame someone else if things go bad. Their noted for that. Oh, is that so said the Captain looking askance at Master Chief Gentlemen where are you staying tonight? We don't have a place yet replied the captain. Well then, I would recommend Jenjen Its just down the road from here. When you get to the end take a right and it's the last building on the right. You can't miss it will have a blue lantern out front. She provides food drink and a place to stay. She's also is the entertainer, she sings. The chief and five look at each other with a quizzical look. The chief says what's singing? Bernardo Din laughs and says singing is like talking except it put to music and she keeps the beat of the music with her words and voice. You don't sing where you come from? No, we don't our voices are not capable of it. Oh sorry, I think you will enjoy it any way. I will send the ferryman for you in the morning his name is kharon. He'll transport you to the Ferugie base. Thank you for the information and the invitation to the Ferugie. My pleasure gentlemen. I must warn you though the Ferugie don't like strangers. They are very unpredictable and Peritus is the worst of the bunch He seems to have a very high ability to read people and if he has any inkling that you are not honest with him, he will kill you instantly. They don't take prisoners as a general way of operating. We understand and thanks again for the warning. The captain digs into his pouch and pulls out a shiny golden credit and lays it on the showcase. Bernardo Din hands him the gun and the box of bullets with the sling. Bernardo opens the door and says don't terry on the way, it's getting near the darkness and it becomes very dangerous on the streets now.

They walk down the stairs and start down the street. Master Chief hold up a minute as the Captain takes off his coat and sticks his arms through both holes made by the sling and slips it over his head. He opens the little door of the gun and puts six bullets in the chamber rotating the cylinder after each bullet seats. He closes the door and holsters the gun under his left arm. He puts his coat on and the gun is completely covered. Captain why did you buy that thing. This Master chief is a very rare Colt 1873 birds head handle revolver chambered in.45 caliber long Colt with 180 grain hollow point bullets. This gun will knock down and kill just about anything that walks. Sir how do you know all this? Well if you remember on earth when we got the knife from Dick, he had one in his case just like this one. I saw it was odd looking so I asked him about it. He told me everything I just told you. It's just what we need on a mission like this. That's why I was so interested in this Bernardo Din along with the fact he seems to know a lot about these Ferugie. By the way what did you think of him? I think he was high born and that he is very smart. I don't know if I completely trust him Why? A person high born like him doesn't need to be way out in the frontier buying and selling arms and liquor. Something happened somewhere that forced him into this life style. That makes me think something is amiss somewhere and I don't think we want to find out what it is. He's very strange to me. I don't know I agree there's just something I can't get a handle on. Let's get going here. Sir I just hope you don't have a reason to use that thing. I hope so to Master Chief.

WALKING DOWN THE MAIN
ROAD IN PANKU PEKU

WELL MASTER CHIEF I don't think Bernardo Din has a very good opinion of us? I picked that up sir, but does he have a point? Is that why Ambassador Iz is with us? And Are the Ferugie really what were here for? Or are we on a scouting mission for the Two-star systems to dominate? I can't answer that question Master Chief, I would hope that we are really here to get rid of the Ferugie and stop them as a menace to the entire galactic system. Master Chief, what do you make of Shamus? I don't know strange little fellow, but he sure knows a lot about whiskey and Gold. How's that? Well did you know there were three types of gold, I didn't? His knowledge of whiskey is second to none, he can tell you everything about where it's made and how it's made just by smelling it.

Just then a man walked out in front of them holding a small disruptor hand weapon. He was dressed in old distressed clothing that didn't fit very well. He said "Good evening gentlemen, I would like to relieve you of your heavy burden of money pouches? Waving the disruptor around as he spoke. I don't think so said Master Chief. Just then they smelled a putrid odor from behind them. A large beast of an animal was standing there almost twice as tall as the Captain and very heavy. He stood on two fat legs with long fat arms that had three fingers with large curved claws. The man in front said this is my friend he is an argolian sloth that loves fresh meat. He generally holds his meat, in this case you two in one arm as he twists the arms and legs off and eats them slowly saving the head for last. I strongly suggest you hand over your pouches and we will be on our way. The Captain looked at master chief and motioned with his eyes for him to move over a bit. Master Chief said hold on there fellow I'll get my purse out no need for violence. As he stepped aside two steps. With this he opened his coat a little and pretended to fumble with his pouch. Hurry up the man said. Sir you've gotten me so nervous I can't get my fingers to work well just hold on. He stepped a little more sideways and as he pretended to get his pooch, he grabbed the Sa on his sash and came down with a viscous slash. The Sa stuck with a tremendous force. The blade cutting deeply into the skull and down across the mans face taking off his nose and upper lip down to his lower lip and into his neck and upper right arm. The man grabbed his face and let out a loud whaling howl as he dropped to his knees and then to the ground on his side.

While this was happening, the Captain turned to his left dropped to his knee and pulled the.45 Colt from its holster. As he swung around the colt came out with the hammer cocked. The sloth stood there in amazement as all of this was happening so fast. The Colt fired, with the first bullet striking him in the chest just above his waist with the bullet traveling upward through him tearing out the base of his heart and thru the upper lobe of his lung. The large arm and paw came whistling over the captain's head knocking off his hat. The second shot went up through the lower jaw of the beast through the top of his open mouth into the brain cavity and exiting through the top of his head. He was dead before he hit the ground on his back the altercation lasted only a few seconds with both assailants laying dead on the ground. The smoke from the Colt blew away and the Captain just looked at the gun. Master Chief came up and said "well I guess what you were told was the truth. I haven't seen such damage done with such a small weapon in a long time" Your right Master Chief as he looked down at the man on the ground.

They both looked around and not a person could be seen. Let's get out of here before somebody gets interested in the noise here. That's a good idea, since there's no law here there's no one to report this incident to. They started walking done the road again with both weapons in plain sight.

JENJENS

BOTH MEN WALKED to the end of the dirty road and turned right. They could see the blue light over the door. There was a strange sound coming from inside. Rather soft and melodious and not unkindly to the ear. They walked into a smoke-filled room with about a dozen persons inside. It looked like a convention of all the races of the galaxy inside. Only one or two turned and looked at the strangers that just came in. A lady was singing from a small stage that had several musicians around it as the lights were shown on her. She was medium height with long white hair that covered her head. She wore a long red dress that sparkled as the light shown on her. She swayed back and forth in rhythm with the music. The Captain and Master Chief couldn't understand the language she used, then they noticed everyone had a universal translator box hung around their necks. Soon the music stopped and Jenjen came down off of the stage. She spotted them immediately and came right up to them. The Captain said good evening and she responded the same. She said how can I help you gentlemen? Master Chief said my name is Chief and this is five and we liked your music. That's nice to hear, she said" I haven't seen you in here before". No, we just arrived, we were sent by Bernardo Din. He said you could put us up for the night. She eyed them up and down and said of course. What do you want? First of all, we would like two of your local solarian ales. Red or blue she asks, blue I think would do just fine. Then we would like a room with two steam environmental boxes. I'll have the room made up while you enjoy the ales. That would be fine, how much? One gold credit will work for the whole thing she said. The Captain pulled out the gold credit and gave it to her and Master Chief pulled out a silver credit and placed it in her hand with a big smile and said this is for you the brightest evening star. She looked at him and smiled and said flattery will get you nothing, but it's nice to hear as she walked away. They sipped their ales and looked around at the boisterous atmosphere as Jenjen moved from table to table talking with each customer. Every time she smiles and says hello, they buy another drink. She's a classy lady you don't see much of these days. You've got to love it. Let's not spend too much time here I think we'll have a long day tomorrow. I think your right captain.

They made their way to their room and found it small, but clean and the two environmental chambers were all set up. They turned them on and almost immediately the warm steam and air mixture started billowing out. They got undressed and entered the chambers and closed the see-through covers down. Breathing deeply and relaxed they slept well.

KHARON

I T SEEMED LIKE they had just fallen asleep when the light in the room changed and woke them up. The lights had come on automatically Master Chief got up and proceeded to get dressed shortly thereafter the captain woke up and got dressed as well. They were just getting their tunics on when a rap on the door alerted them someone was outside. Just a minute Master Chief yelled out. As the captain strapped on the colt, checked to see it was all loaded and put his coat on to cover it up. Master Chief grabbed his Sa and gently opened the door. A tall figure was standing there. He was dressed in all black with a long coat that reached almost to the floor. He had a long full hood over his head. He was slightly stooped over and he had a long black staff in his hand. In a deep voice that sounded like it came from a deep pit he announced his name. I'm Kharon, I've come to fetch you gentlemen as directed by Bernardo Din. I will carry you across the Styx to Beta. They couldn't really see his face, but he was a daunting figure just standing there. Master

Chief said we'll be right with you as he put his coat and hat on. The captain already had his hat on and his hands were covered.

Kharon just turned and moved away. It didn't look like he was walking as most people do. He just seemed to float don the corridor to the exit. The captain and master chief just looked at each other and followed him. Once they were outside the morning was cool and the constant blue light shown as it was hidden behind the horizon. They walked behind Kharon as he moved down a well-worn path. So, they were going down a slight incline and came upon a craft next to a small tree line. The craft was a boat type of vehicle with both ends being the same highly raked upward with a long stem on each end. There were seats on both sides of the craft and Kharon got in first. He turned to them and said take a seat wherever you want. The master chief said which end is the bow and which is the stern? Kharon replied that those terms were unknown to him He stood in the middle and placed the metal end of his staff into a small box. He pushed the staff forward and the craft began to move forward. He then moved the staff to the left and the craft turned slightly right and away from the tree line. There was no nose as the craft moved into to the light mist that had come up from the shore line.

The captain asked Kharon how far was it to the beta shore line. Karon said not to long that they would be there shortly. Master chief said what's propelling this craft. Kharon just looked his way and said hat it runs on the energy produced by the people riding in the craft. All people have an energy field about them, that can't be seen but it's there. The craft senses the energy and uses it to move thru space. Quite efficient don't you think? Yes, I would say so as long as the people are alive. Quit right he stated and turned away. The master chief and the captain just looked at each other and shrugged. After a short ride Kharon announced that they were almost there. Master chief and the captain looked up and couldn't see through the fog, but soon a black mass was right in front of them. The craft slowed down and was drifting to a small dock that jutted out. Kharon brought the craft to a stop and he said this was Beta. Master chief said how much do we owe you? Kharon shrugged and said the standard fee, two pieces of silver apiece. Master chief dug into his pouch and handed him four silver credits. They got out and turned and asked how do we call you when we want to come back. Kharon just pointed with his staff and said ring the bell twice and I will appear. He placed the staff in the small box and pulled it back towards him the craft soon disappeared into the mist.

BETA

THE MIST WAS starting to roll away as they walked up a pathway. They rounded a corner and they saw a large stone wall facing them. It was at least three men tall made out of large stones that were black with tiny flecks of a silvery material. The stones were fit tightly together with no mortar or any kind of bonding agent visible. They moved forward and saw a large open gate. There was no one guarding the gate or anyone around as they passed through. Master Chief looked at the captain and said "this place gives me the shivers" I know exactly how you feel. My question is with a fortress this size why isn't there anyone patrolling the gate area. Let's keep a good eye out. They passed through the gate and stopped to take in what they were seeing. On the inside of the walled area was a grassy area. They could barely make out another gate and high wall. As they moved forward the Captain noticed a small building made of stone the their left. He motioned to master chief and they slowly walked over to the small building in the shadows of the huge wall. As they came up to it, they saw it was very short, but had a tall angled roof. It was set down into the ground and had a large heavy door. The door was locked, but a small twist of iron was under the handle. Master Chief twisted the key and they pulled open the door. It made a slight squeak as it came open. They both looked around and still no one was there. The Captain went in first followed closely behind by Master Chief. He pulled the door closed and it was completely dark inside. As the Captain moved in a step the lights came on startling the both of them. Must be on a motion sensor or something. As their eyes adjust to the darkness, they could see a large number of wooden boxes stacked along the left-hand wall. On the right-hand side was a four wheeled cart type of object standing on its side. The floor had ruts carved into it and it was obvious the cart wheels would fit into the ruts. Master Chief went to the cartons and opened one. He saw about a dozen objects that resembled a ball in each section of the box. They weren't round, but oblong with both ends pointed, but not sharp. He held one out and looked at a closely. In the middle was a round button type of protrusion with a lever attached to it. He pushed the button and the lever turned to three different positions each marked with one line two lines or three lines. He pushed the lever back to straight up and released the button. He handled the object and then smelled it. Chief what have you got there? asked the captain. Well sir its what I call a hand bomb. It's made to throw and when you release the button this lever is a timer and it goes off. It smells like thermite. I would say these are very powerful and will cause a lot of damage and a large fire ball, not the least of which will create a lot of noise and blinding light. Very deadly and there's enough of these to start and finish a small war. He handed one to the Captain. Are these safe? Yes sir, as long as you don't press the button in the middle and then release it without adjusting the timer. That's the little lever attached to it. Also notice the button is magnetized so you can push it in set the lever, release it and attach it to anything that has ferrous metal in it. Quit ingenious rally.

Chief I'm going to walk down the cave here and see where it leads. You take an inventory of what's stored here. Aye sir, don't get lost! The chief counted the boxes and looked to see how many were in each box. He also found detonators that had their own timers built in. The Chief looked to his right and saw a heavily built cart with four wheels leaning against the wall. It was heavy and it took all of his strength to tip it on its wheels. The wheel size matched the grooves cut into the stone floor. He maneuvered the cart over to the groves and they matched perfectly. He heard something and looked up to see the captain coming back to the storage area. Well what did you find? This tunnel goes all the way down and around to the elevator to the landing pad. They must use this as a storage area for ammunition and fuel storage. Wow that's dangerous. Yes, there are large storage tanks full of fuel for the ship and thrustor fuel let's get out of here before someone finds us in here. The chief handed the captain several of the hand bombs. What am I going to do with these he said? Well stick them into the small pockets in the inside of your coat. Each side has three pockets for emergencies like this. The Captain put two in each pocket on both sides of his coat, while the chief did the same.

They exited the small storage building and looked around at the wall. No one was around so they began walking towards the second wall and gate. As they walked up to the gate, they crossed a small bridge and looked up. This was another massive stone wall like the first one except the gate was slightly smaller. The gate was made of heavy timbers with a large metal sliding bar that was slipped all the way to the left on the left-hand door.

THE FERUGIE COMPOUND

As soon as they entered the gate, they were stopped by two Ferugie guards carry long poles with a large curved blade at the end. It looked like one half of a Sa. The guards were dressed in silver breast plates heavy black tunics underneath the breast plate and heavy black gloves. They had on dark colored pants tucked into black boots that came half way to their fat knees. They had a universal translator box around their necks. On the breast plates was an emblem embossed with a round circle and two suns on it with a small black planet in the middle of all three circles. The chief said were here to see Peritas. The guards looked at him and noticed he was wearing his Sa on his sash. The Captain kept his head down and they waved them forward.

This building was a large hall type of structure with high ceiling and a lot of flowing light-colored fabrics hung from the heavy timbers. It had high stone walls with windows near the top where the ceiling meets the walls. Hanging in the back of the hall was a large golden emblem hung from the ceiling it had the same rings with two sun type of planets inside of them with a small back planet in the middle of it all. There were over a hundred Ferugie milling about. All dressed in brightly colored clothing made up of pants tunics and boots. Most of all though they all had at least four arms that hung past their waists. Some had five arms and a couple had a small fifth arm that was not quite developed. As soon as the chief and the captain were noticed they started to come forward to view the strangers. The loud clicking of there teeth was very alarming and the chief automatically went for his Sa. The captain stuck his hand into his coat and felt the reassuring birds head handle of his colt. They both stood their ground as the Ferugie got closer trying not to show any fear.

All of a sudden, the Ferugie stopped moving and a commotion was beginning to build in the back of the crowd. The crowd split and put there heads down with their eye tucked into its socket. An imposing figure approached. He was dressed in a blue tunic with blue pants tucked into highly polished black boots. He wore a golden breast plate with the same circled figure emblazoned on it. He had six arms and each had a highly polished Sa in his hands. The Sa's were twirling at high speed as each arm moved indecently from the other. His wide mouth was open showing large white triangular teeth. He also wore a universal translator around his neck.

When he got up to the two men he stopped. The whistling of the Sas in the air made a tell-tale sound never before heard by the Chief and the Captain. After a bit of time the impressive display stopped and he walked forward. The chief said Peritas I assume. Peritas' eye jumped back and forth and he finally said in a low gruff voice You may call me emperor. And who might you be? My name is Chief and this is five. The captain looked up and nodded making eye contact with Peritas. The Captain said we've come looking for work and we were told you might have jobs that would interest us. Peritas looked him up and down, who sent you? We initially heard of you form a Centalorian named Lucius. We then again heard from Bernardo Din that you might have something available. Peritas looked both of them thoroughly and said what type of work interest you? Well we can do just about anything? Peritas left hand reached out and pulled back the Chiefs coat lightly and saw the Sa. He asked where did you get that? The chief said the previous owner tried to kill me with it and so when I killed him, I took it. Humm Peritas said and what about you looking at the Captain. He held up his right hand revealing the five fingers and said I'll do what's necessary. Everyone was taken aback by the sight of these two strangers that obviously had seen combat before and were not impressed with flashy shows. Peritas said maybe I could find something for you in the slave compound on Terra Alpha. The chief said I don't know of this place where is it? It's in the Tuberon system not far from here. What's the pay? asked the Captain. Peritas looked offended and his eye jumped around. He said the pay is five gold credits per ship that trades with us. That is if I don't decide to kill you first. Now why would you do that? asked the Chief. Because I can, said, Peritas and I think you two were responsible for the killing of my agents in Panku Peku the other night. You mean the little man and his Argolian sloth worked for you. Yes, I get a cut of everything they take in. They tried to rob us and threatened to kill us. So, said Peritas that's what they do. Well said the

Captain I think we will decline your offer of work and leave now. I don't think so said Peritas. I think I will kill you and feed you to my staff.

The Chief and the Captain looked at each other and the Chief took two steps to the right of the Captain. The group of Ferugie got agitated and started to move forward. The Chief pulled his Sa and cut down the nearest Ferugie with a violent and swift move. The Captain dropped to one knee and pulled the Colt he fired the first shot at Peritas, which caught him right in the middle of the breast plate in the center of the emblazoned image. The bullet crashed thorough the Ferugie sending him flying backward. The Ferugie standing directly behind Peritas also went down as the bullet passed through him. The Captain fired again at the nearest Ferugie. Taking each one down as he fired. All six-armed Ferugie went down before anyone knew what had happened. The Chief yelled "cover your eyes" as he threw two hand bombs in quick succession into the back of the crowd. The explosions were deafening the bright light of the thermite explosion blinded everyone not covered up. The captain stood up and threw two bombs, to the left and they went off almost immediately. The hall was erupting in flame as the wall and ceiling hangings quickly caught fire. The Chief set and rolled two bombs into the panicked crowd. The Captain did the same. Now it was just mayhem within the crowd. The anguished cries of the dyeing and wounded echoed throughout the building. The Captain said let's get out of here. The smoke was settling to the floor and it was very hard to see anything. The Chief and the Captain ran for the first gate. When they got to the gate, they each threw two more bombs and stepped thru the gate. They slammed the gate shut. The Chief said hold on as he held the button on a bomb against the large metal slide. He felt the slide move as he pulled it across the door. They turned and ran across the bridge and saw two Ferugie guards running towards them the chief yelled out ASSISSANS, ASSISSANS and pointed toward the gate. The two guards ran past them and as they did the Chief pulled out his last bomb and rolled it up the bridge. They both turned away as the bombs went off. They continued to run down the path to the last gate.

The Captain stopped and said this way pointing towards the little stone house. The Chief said I don't really think we have time for this Captain. He just smiled and said there aren't any more guards and this won't take long. They got to the house and opened the door. The captain said fill the cart with the crates of thermite bombs and a detonator. I'll check to make sure the way is clear. He ran down the cave and turned the corner. The Captain came to the large storage tanks of fuel. He pulled his knife and jabbed the knife into the flexible hoses used to fuel the space craft. Immediately the fuel started to spill out and run down the floor in all directions. The Captain ran back to the small stone house with his tunic over his nose and mouth. The Chief could smell the fumes from the fuel. The cart was brimming full of bombs and a detonator. The Captain said let's go before the fumes kill us. The chief pushed two mall buttons on the front of the cart and the cart moved slowly at first but then picked up speed as they went out the door of the stone house. The Chief closed the door and twisted the lock. Both men took a moment to catch their breath before moving towards the gate

They looked back at the compound that was totally engulfed in flames. The high timbered ceiling was fully ablaze and starting to crumble. Let's get going as they both ran out of the last gate heading for the dock. I hope Kharon is near by or we could be brunt to a crisp also. "Said the Chief". They ran to the dock and rang the bell twice as instructed. Nothing happened as they watched the blaze keep burning and spreading to other buildings in the compound. Then a low rumble shook the ground. They both looked at each other and the Chief rang the bell again. Shortly a faint light appeared in the mist. And the craft came into sight. They ran to the dock and jumped in before it stopped. Kharon said in his deep voice "what's going on and why the fireworks in the compound'? I don't know, but take us to the space port please. Kharon punched the staff forward and they moved into the dark mist. They both just sat there with their heads down breathing deeply. The exertion from the running and the light atmosphere took its 'toll on them. Finally, Master Chief says 'sir we're getting to old for this sort of thing. I agree Master Chief next time remind me to send one of the ensigns. Sir there will be no next time". The glowing in the sky could be seen all the way to the space port. As they docked Master Chief gave Kharon his bag of silver credits and said. "It's time to retire old man and good luck" They both jumped off the craft heading towards the space port. The AI rolled up and said your craft is ready gentlemen. Thank you said the Captain and handed the AI, his bag of gold credits, as they entered the STX. The AI said you can't leave until Bernardo Din says its okay. We'll leave anyway and give Bernardo Din the bag. The STX lifted gently off and turned all the way around and took off.

IN FRONT OF BERNARDO DINS EMPORIUM

BERNARDO DIN AND Shamus were standing in front of the store looking at the large bright orange glow in the sky over Beta. Shamus asked "what's going on and why the orange sky?" I don't know said Bernardo, but nothing good comes from a color like that. I think he Ferugie compound is on fire. A strange larger glow came from the area of the space port near the compound. Then a rolling vibration in the ground and finally the sound of a large explosion. Several smaller thunderous sounds came rolling thru. Shamus I think the whole compound is destroyed and probably the Ferugie with it. I think your right sire, I wonder what happened to those two strange men that were in asking about the Ferugie and the work they wanted? Shamus I think those two men are the cause of all of this mayhem. Sire do you think they were assassins? Bernardo smirked and nodded no and said I don't think they were assassins, but I do think they were men fully capable of close armed combat, probably very proficient at it. Sire, do you think they were caught up in it the conflagration? No, I think they were two smart for that, at least I hope so I rather liked them. I agree sire Chief was very knowledgeable about whiskey.

Just then Kharon floats up to them. Kharon what's going on? Sire I took the two men to Beta as you requested. They weren't there long and they rang the bell again. I noticed the fire at the compound and asked them about it? They didn't say much they were out of breath from running, I guess. They requested me to take them to the space port and I did. When we got there Chief gave me this whole bag of silver credits. I told him my fee is always two silver credits. He said don't worry take it and retire. Sire what a strange thing to say. They proceeded to their craft and immediately took off. Sire what does retire mean? It means that you don't work any more that you rest and do other things you want to do that you never had time for before. Kharon just shrugged a little bit and turned and left the area with his shiny black staff and a bag full of silver credits.

Shamus I don't think he understands? No sire he doesn't, you see he doesn't understand work. He has always been a ferryman and he always will be. Bernardo Din looked puzzled and said I don't understand? Sire Kharon is death. Are you saying were dead? Oh no sire we're alive you see he never looked at us in the eyes. Only when he looks you in your eyes are you dead. Shamus I don't understand the ways of the netherworld. I know sire that's why I'm here to help you.

They both just looked at the sky for a moment and the little AI rolled up from the space port. He came up to

Bernardo and held out his grappling arm with a large bag in it. He said "sire this is for you," Bernardo took it and opened the bag to see it was filled with golden credits. AI said "sire Five told me to give this to you and he said thanks a lot for your help. Bernardo had a strange look on his face and said where did they go. AI turned and pointed into the sky away from the orange glow. There sire I told them not to leave until you gave them permission, but they just ignored me. No problem AI they are just that type of beings. They generally do what they want or what their ordered to do. Yes, sire as he turned and rolled away. Just as Bernardo was going to look away, he saw two golden streaks and then two explosions in the sky. Bernardo said I think were going to need two new guard buoys. Yes, sire said Shamus. Then a strange sliver of light in the sky came on and shortly went out. Sire, what was that? I should have known Shamus, I should have known. Known what sire? That STX craft they came in was to small to have made it all the way here on its own. It didn't carry enough fuel to came all this way from any of the nearest ports. That Shamus was a mother ship. That's how they got here. Sire it didn't show up on any of our sensors for deep space. They must have some ort of shield around it or cloaking device. Shamus looked at his wrist screen and said sire, I just got notified that the galactic navigation council has just issued a new waypoint. So, what does that have to do with us? Sire the waypoint is named PAAG. And it's about out there pointing with his finger to where they saw the sliver of light.

Shamus I think its time we consider setting up shop in a new location.

But where sire and why? Because I think this place is going to get a lot more attention than we've had before and it's the kind I don't want. I think we should look at the other side of the frontier maybe over by the Sagurius system I here there's some nice places where the weather is more conducive for our older bones. They both turned and started walking into the emporium. Shamus I'll stand you to a flagon of ale as we plan out our new adventure, shaking the bag of gold in his hand. Yes, sire I'm always up for a flagon of ale.

IN THE SHUTTLE BAY
OF THE EXCALIBUR

THE BAY DOORS opened and the claxon went off. The STX was just in sight and heading in on final approach. The little ship came in and settled in next to the shuttle. The doors opened and the decontamination portal moved up and attached so they could get out and go directly into the decontamination camber. As they came out the other end the crewmen took their coats and hats. The first officer was their and meet them along with the doctor and the Chief Engineer She said you two look terrible I want both of you to get to your quarters and get into your environmental chambers for a while. The Captain and Master chief just said yes mam thank you for that medical advice. The Captain stopped and said "first officer I want an officers call when were rested and rehabbed in my conference room. The captain handed the chief engineer his birds head handled

Colt along with on of the hand bombs; Chief Engineer handle these carefully they both contain explosive devices. Let me know what you think.? Aye sire will do, by the way welcome back. Thank you replied the captain as they walked off.

OFFICERS CALL IN THE CONFERENCE ROOM

THE CAPTAIN AND Master Chief walked in with fresh uniforms and the captain had on the empty holster for the colt. Everyone stood up and clapped when they entered. They both just sat down and said thank you.

The captain said plot find the Tuberon system. I'm looking for a small planet with two suns call Terra Alpha. Aye sir. Navigation and helm when you get the coordinates head for it. They both responded aye sir. The chief engineer put the colt on the table and passed it around so everyone could see it. Sir that's a fine piece. Very old school in design and function, but relatively new build. The metal work is heavy iron, steel with minor alloys. Well built for close quarters combat, but not very good at far range. How did it work? With a raised eyebrow. Very well Chief Engineer it took down and Argolian sloth and six Ferugie with out a problem. But your right in very close quarters. Commander Volarian spoke up. Sir you were supposed to be on a recon mission not a full-fledged fire fight. We were very worried about you especially when Beta caught fire and destroyed itself. You were supposed to call us in if anything went wrong. I know Commander, my apologies, but everything got out of hand very fast and we just did what came naturally. Sir what happened?

Well we meet with Bernardo Din, I bought the birds head colt, we went to a place to stay the night, Its very dangerous at night there. That's where we met up with a man and his Argolian Sloth that tried to rob us and we dispatched them and got off the street. We mt Kharon in the morning and he took us to Beta. Sir I hate to interrupt you, but we were watching all the time and there was no life form with you when you went to Beta. Well Commander I can't explain what you didn't see, but Kharon was real and he had a strange craft that took us to Beta and brought us back to the space port.

Chief engineer what did you find out about the hand bomb? Well sir it's a thing of beauty. Well designed and assembled. The shape with both ends tapered like that, make it very efficient to throw. Very aerodynamic in an atmosphere. I bet you could throw this a long way and very accurately. The thermite itself is highly advanced, probably better than what we have. Very hot burning, very fast burning giving off a lot to light and red-hot fragments from the casing. The trigger is the best part, easy to use, magnetic to be able to attach to any ferrous metal and highly regulated. The switching bar allows three timing events giving you room to move away and time to throw it. Overall very efficient, I'll be using this design and material in all future devices we make.

Sensors what is your take on Beta? Sir there are no life forms down there now. The compound is completely destroyed. All that's left are the stone walls everything else is gone. The space port next to it is destroyed along with the ship that was on it. I think it was the Columbine that Lucius told us about. There is nothing there to reconstitute any kind of force against us. Sir just for the record all life forms showed up except for the one you called kharon. Thank you I agree with your assessment. All of the Ferugie are dead, except for any that are on this Terra Alpha and the ones in custody with the galactic court.

Sir yes, plot, Terra Alpha located and the course is laid in, very well let's get going.

Commander Volarian when we get to Terra Alpha, I want you on the outside of us to block their view in case they have a sensor array. Aye sir, Major Pike your men will take the lead on this operation. Yes sir, thank you sir.

ENROUTE TO THE TUBERON SYSTEM

CAPTAIN ON THE bridge came the call as the captain came into the bridge and took his chair. Sir everything is running normally and Chief engineer said that we might be able to start the magneto flux drive system if we get closer. The Turberon system is very near the dividing line between the frontier and the galactic systems. That will be a pleasure if we can finally start building up some speed. Tell the chief engineer to get the reactor down to temperature as we get closer. Aye sir. Captain Comms here just got a message from Commander Risig on the MaryAnne, they made it to the galactic court on Centurri 2 after a brief stop at Tripar to bury the Terra Formers men. The Captain just shook his head and said I should have known she would do something like that. Well sir you didn't say she couldn't stop there. The Captain just glared at Comms. He put his head down and started to work on his equipment.

Captain the Chief engineer would like to see you in the engineering bay. Fine I'll be right down.

ENGINEERING BAY

CHIEF ENGINEER YOU wanted to see me. Ah yes sir, I could have come up to the bridge. That's okay I need the walk anyways. Yes sir, I've got your projectiles for you. He handed him a bin with individual slots for a number of bullets he created. Sir these are pretty fragile. You don't want to bang them around a lot. They are exact replicas of what you gave me. They are dimensionally perfect as we can get them here out of the replicator. The cases are a brass alloy we developed based on the originals. The projectiles themselves are an alloy similar to lead, we don't have that onboard, but they'll react the same way. The powder is the same, very flammable and confined in the cartridge will explode just like the originals. The little cap in the middle of the base was the hardest to replicate. It contains fulminated mercury. That's un-heard of here or on Asanti. I've replicated it as best as I can. When I get back to base, I'll be able to get it almost exact. These will still work sir, but probably sound a bit different. No problem Chief I appreciate your efforts. Thank you, sir I appreciate your saying that. Its always interesting being around you and Master Chief. Sir if you don't mind me saying he's been acting kind of funny lately, since you've been back. How so Chief Engineer? I can't put my finger on its sir just kind of quiet like he's got something on his mind. Well Chief Engineer I'll tell you this that mission took a lot out of all of us. In- fact this whole mission has been as tough as I've ever been on. I think it's this damned Frontier. I've never seen anything so black and desolate as this place. I think it's the lack of light and nothing to orient to like the stars. Especially for older guys like us. I agree with you sir, when I was on the shuttle bay deck and looked out. I don't know how those young Marines did that intra ship transfer. That scared the hell out of me just looking out there much less having to jump into that abyss. I agree Chief is it our age? Maybe be sir maybe. Captain to the bridge, Captain to the bridge. I've got to go Chief thanks again great job. Than you sir.

ON THE BRIDGE

CAPTAIN ON THE bridge. Captain we've entered the Tuberon system, no sight of Terra Alpha. Very good Sensors anything out there? Aye sir, but way off should I give them a full scan? No just passive for now I don't want to alert them if our position. Commander Valerian bring the Fang up high and close. Aye Sir. Major Pike get your marines on alert Aye sir. Master Chief to the bridge. Helm as we get into range of Terra Alpha I want to go into an equatorial orbit, standard distance Aye sir.

Ah, Master Chief good to see you how are doing? Very good sir, took me a bit of time to get all of that smoke and dust from Panku Peku out of my system. Good we should be getting some indications of this Terra Alpha that Peritas talked about.

Sensors to Captain, sir we've got that little planet system you wanted coming up on the imager. Good put it up and let's see what we've got. Aye sir. A fuzzy image started to appear and with several attempts to focus it finally came into view. Sir, it's got two small suns about 45 degrees off center from the planet. Standard mixture of silicon, carbon, nitrogen and some small amounts of trace elements. Looks pretty standard elemental wise. The size of these systems out here is really amazing. All small and very different from what we find in the standard star systems. Why is that sir? Sensors, I don't know, but I think it has to do with the frontier itself. It seems that everything we've found out here is just the remains of star formation as a whole. I think this is just the remains of when the galaxy first came into existence. With no gravity out here to hold everything together this is just the remnants of star formation. That's my theory and I'm going to stick to it, until someone can prove me wrong. I'll take your explanation sir. Sir looks like there's a small ship orbiting the planet. *Red alert Red Alert.* All hands to battle stations. Were coming in on them fast sir. Helm slow us down to enter orbit. Aye sir. Slowing down to trans orbital speed.

Sir a shuttle craft is coming up to the orbiting ship. Weapons target both ships but hold fire. Aye sir weapons on full lock. Sensors get a good scan on both ships, Aye sir. Sensors are they Ferugie? Negative sir life forms indicate they are some form of Ninvarta a species out of the Pelota system. A long way from home sir. I'll say, have they gone to any kind of alert status? No sir they seem to be breaking orbit and heading out. I think we scared them off. Very good, cancel red alert enter standard orbit. Aye sir. Plot to Captain-go ahead, sir I would recommend that we move to a 40 degree above equatorial orbit. This will give us a lot shorter rout to the settlement below. Sounds good go to the recommended orbit Aye sir.

Sir settlement is coming into view, put it up on the imager. Can we get a closer view sensor? Aye sir try this. The settlement came in closer so they could see the buildings and topography of the land around the settlement. Nothing but desert sir, any other settlements on the planet or signs of habitation? Negative sir I'll do a penetrating scan that should go down a good way into the planets crust. I wonder if anything is below surface since the surface is pretty rough.

Major Pike are you getting this imagery? Yes, sir looks pretty small and desolate. I agree, but don't underestimate the Ferugie. Remember this is their territory. The settlement came into view with a series of mud type houses and small buildings. The compound was a fortress looking structure with gates at both ends with high walls and guard towers on each corner. Inside the compound were several larger buildings and small structures at both ends. Sensors can you make out any of the inhabitants of the fortress? Negative sir not individually. There are a group of life forms in the larger building concentrated into groups maybe 10-15 per group. They seem to be all kinds all mixed in together. Sir one small building has 3-4 individuals in it, look to be Ferugie, based on the parameters we have from the captives.

Captain, what's your take on this? Major this looks like a slave compound based on the current analysis. I would guess the Ferugie in the one building are either guards or some type of administrative force. Based on what we got from Bernardo Din and Peritas the Ferugie us mercenaries here along with their own people. Captain what do you want to do? Major I want this to be your operation not mine. I'm going to let you formulate the battle pan and then you can execute it. Thank you, sir thank, you. Don't thank me yet Major this is not going to be any kind of cake walk. I think I would rather face the Ferugie, at least you know how they think and what they are going to do within reason. Mercenaries are a whole different story. You never know how hard their going to fight and what their motivation is. Very asymmetrical. Yes, sir I'll alert the men and form a plan. I'll get back to you when we are ready. Very good Major.

Captain do you really think this is a good idea? Well Master Chief we all have to get our feet wet sometime and it's about time the Major did, yes sir but this could get complicated, I don't know if he has ever formulated and then carried out an attack from space before. I know, but we will be here to help if he gets into a real problem. Sir, I'll be happy to go down and fly the shuttle craft and watch out for my boys. Well Master Chief I've never heard of you calling Marines "your boys" are you going soft on Marines. Not a bit sir, but I do feel some responsibility for them. That's okay Master Chief, lets see what he comes up with. I always have veto power. Yes sir.

TERRA ALPHA

CAPTAIN-I'VE GOT THE plan. Go ahead Major. Sir I want to take two shuttles down each with marines. We'll attack both gates at the same time. Breach the gates and storm the compound. We will fire only if fired upon, we'll release the prisoners and take the mercs. The Ferugie will take prisoners if they don't give up, we'll do what's necessary to protect ourselves.

That's it pretty simple really. We'll Major you can count on the Ferugie not giving up. They will fight to the last man. We've learned that from our previous encounters. I would assume you will have to kill them, so get that straight in your head before you go. Yes sir. Your plan sounds decent, I'll throw in a sensor blast when you're ready to breach. That will give you some time and a bit of a distraction. Major I like distractions as you might have noticed. Yes, sir I'll take whatever you can give us. Very well Major get ready to go. Aye sir.

Sir I'll fly the shuttle if you don't mid. Thanks Master Chief, but I would prefer the shuttle bay ensign to fly it. He needs the experience and I want you to be the back up go to guy. Get the STX ready to launch, but only if they get into trouble. The Chief just smiled and left the bridge.

Doctor, have your team assemble in the shuttle bay in case we have causalities. Aye sir. Sir do you think its wise to not let the Master Chief go on this mission. Doctor, I think its time to let other people carry some of the load around here. Master Chief and I need to share our experience and knowledge. I think it's time. So, do I Captain, so do I. Anyways I've come to realize that and I think the Master Chief will get used to it over time.

ON THE GROUND ON
TERRA ALPHA

B OTH SHUTTLES CAME in through the thin atmosphere then split up as the settlement came into view. They landed a short distance away from each gate of the compound hidden by small hills. The Marines piled out and took up defensive positions around the shuttle craft. Each Marines was dressed in a tight-fitting light brown environmental suit. They had on tight fitting helmets that contained their communications gear and full-face shields. The material on the suits changed color based on their background. The change was almost instantaneous as they moved from shadow to light and back again.

They carried short barreled disruptors. Hand disruptors for close combat and a knife strapped upside down on their shoulders. Two Marines one on each shuttle carried a special build disruptor that had an image intensifier on the top of the barrel. Major Pike ordered each sniper man to clear the guard towers of men and weapons. They both fired almost instantaneously. The golden ray spit out of the barrel and immediately impacted the weapons of the guards in the tower. Once the target tower exploded, they moved to the next tower. All the towers were put out of commission.

Major Pike checked in with everyone and then called out Captain ever one in position hit them with the scanner beam.

Sensors-hit the small building with a focused beam then spread out the beam to cover the entire compound, Aye sir firing now.

Major pike and his team ducked down and a load roar came over them with a big vibration on the ground. Then another softer roar and less vibration. Major pike yelled forward and both teams ran towards the gates. The first wo men placed the charges and the gates fell in on themselves. They rushed in and started there standard clearing sweeps. A few mercenaries came out of the buildings with weapons drawn, but sort of staggered around not focusing on anybody or anything. The marines hit them and secured them to the ground with stakes. The buildings were locked, but nothing the Marines could not handle. They went through buildings and unlocked the cells. The cells were filled with all types of people form around the galaxy. Most were undernourished and dressed in only rags.

Major Pike and a few marines hit the small enclosed room where the sensors had indicated the Ferugie were located. They kicked in the door and the room was in a shamble. They stopped and just stared ahead. The Ferugie were dead what was left of them lay in a heap. They immediately turned and left the room. The prisoners were now out in the open enjoying the freedom and the sunshine.

Some went directly to a watering station and drank their fill before they dropped down and just sat there looking at the marines that freed them. The language barrier was not broken, but the look in their eyes and on their faces showed the great gratitude they had for being unshackled and freed. Some of the prisoners that were in better physical shape went to the guards tied on the ground and began kicking and punching them. One came up with a large piece of wood and delivered several hard blows to the guard's heads and bodies. Soon their prisoners found the strength to join in on the beatings. The marines gathered and just watched.

One marine lieutenant came to Major Pike and asked if they should stop the beatings. Major Pike turned and walked away and said no that they were leaving now and the prisoners will take care of the guards.

Major Pike to Captain. Sir the compound is taken and under the control of the prisoners. I'm returning with my men to the shuttles and then to the Excalibur. Very good Major any causalities or injuries. Noe sir It wasn't much of a fight. Very good major, see you on the Excalibur.

Shortly the shuttles took off leaving the smoking ruin of the compound in their wake.

ONBOARD THE EXCALIBUR

THE SHUTTLES LANDED in quick succession and the marines hurried though the decontamination process. Major Pike exited first and came up to the Captain with a towel in his hand wiping down the last of the decom fluid from his face and hands. Sir everyone accounted for and back on board safely. Very good Major your plan worked out magnificently and everyone came home safe. That's great work you and your men have a lot to be proud of. Thank you, sir, I appreciate your kind words and allowing me to execute my plan. Now where do we go from here? We go home Major, it's been a long and arduous journey and we all need and deserve a rest.

Commander Volarian when your marines get back on board were going to head home. Thank you, sir was looking, forward to it.

Comm this is the Captain tell HQ were done here and heading home Aye sir. Navigation Set the fastest route home. Aye sir. Chief Engineer start the reactor up and get ready to make light speed as soon as we get into galactic territory. Aye sir it will be my pleasure. Plot as soon as you get the coordinates lay them in and be ready to move. Aye sir. Major get your men ready on the shuttle, we'll leave as soon as everyone gets settled. Aye Sir.

The marines piled into the shuttle and both took off as soon as the doors were latched. It wasn't long until the Excalibur's shuttle returned and settled in. The shuttle bay doors closed down and sealed.

CAPTAIN ON THE BRIDGE

HELM PREPARE TO leave orbit. Aye sir. Plot are you set? Aye sir. Comms to Captain-go ahead, sir we've got a priority communication coming in from HQ. Master Chief what do you think they want now? I don't know sir, but I bet it isn't good. Sir HQ advises us that we should go directly to Cellin Yar from here and then return to HQ It seems we have to pick up a scientific team just finishing up there studies there. Cellin Yar did you say? Yes, sir I'll put it up on the imager. The Captain moved his chair over to the gods eye view. Sir that's substantially out of our way. I can see that Plot. Comm did they say why us and not somebody else. No sir they were insistent on us do this. Damn said the Captain why is it always us? The Captain turned towards the Master Chief and he just shrugged his shoulders. Captain, yes Ambassador, how far is it to Cellin Yar and how long will it delay us getting home. It's a bit out of our way and probably will delay us a pretty long while. The Ambassador looked down and shrugged his shoulders. Captain if I may offer a suggestion, go ahead Master Chief. Sir why don't we transfer the Ambassador to the Fang and let them go directly home from here. No sense in dragging the Fang and the Marines all the way to Cellin Yar. Ambassador would you like that. He turned and with a big toothy grin said yes very much Captain it's been a long and tiring voyage that I would appreciate ending as soon as possible. Very good then go pack your bags and be ready to move quickly. Thank you Master Chief. My pleasure sir.

Chief Engineer would you please make arrangements to move the Ambassadors environmental chamber to the Fang as soon as possible. Aye sir. Commander Volarian your going to have a new guest for the trip home. We're transferring the Ambassador to the Fang. You can then go directly home. While we divert to Cellin Yar. No sense keeping you and your Marines out here any longer than necessary. Thank you, sir if you don't think you'll need us any longer? No Commander we should do just fine

Navigation plot a course to Cellin Yar Aye sir, What's Cellin Yar? Navigation is a frozen planet near the Ariotte system. We're going there to pick up a scientific team. Aye Sir. Sir have you been there before. No Nav I've been around some Cribari that used to go there all the time.

Captain this is Commander Villamarin we've gotten the Ambassador on board with his environmental chamber. Were ready to go. Very good Commander have a safe flight back. Commander this is Master Chief, yes Master Chief. Sir I would like to stand you and your marines to a flagon of ale when I return. That's great Master Chief we'll look forward to it. Sir I know a little spot called the Boar and Dragon that would be happy to serve you and your men.

That's a deal Master Chief we'll keep track of your return and meet you there.

Captain the course to Cellin Yar is laid in and were ready to go. Very good helm takes us to Celling Yar.

Both ships move off in their own direction.

ON THE WAY TO CELLIN YAR

CAPTAIN WERE ENTERING the galactic field, we should be able to pick up speed now. Very good helm thank you. Chief Engineer is the reactor ready to take over? Yes, sir indications are we should be able to pick up speed to at least 1.0 light speed. Very good Chief make it happen and keep moving it up to 1.6 as son as possible. Aye sir. Helm take it up slowly until 1.0 light speed very good sir. Helm keep the speed coming up to 1.6 as she takes it on. Yes sir.

Master Chief, what do you think? Sir quite frankly I'm glad the ambassador is gone. I was never really comfortable around him. I never really trusted him. I thought he was a spy. Master Chief interesting observation, I don't think he was a spy, but I never really bought into the idea he was just an observer either, and not really needed in the frontier.

I think there are a lot of other motives at work here. I remember what Bernardo Din said "nothing is ever what it seems when your dealing with governments or politicians" I think that was very good advice. I wonder what he'll do now that the Ferugie are gone? I don't know sir, but I'll bet it has to do with gold, ale or weapons. I agree, I liked him. So, did I. That little guy with him Shamus was a strange little man also. I wonder what he really was? He wasn't human, but he wasn't really any kind of galactic person either. I never ran across anther species like him. Well Master Chief I think you'll have a lot of time to think about it. I agree sir.

Plot to Captain- go ahead plot, sir I've got the Ariotte system up on the imager. Good let's take a look. The Captain moved his chair over to the imager as the galactic system came into focus. Plot-check with Nav and get his coordinates to Cellin Yar. Aye sir coming up. The dotted red line of the proposed route came into focus and that everyone looked to see where they were going. Sir Cellin Yar should be in the middle of the Ariotte system. Very good. Com contact HQ and give them our updated course and ETA into the Ariotte system. Aye Caption. Full speed a ahead gentleman. Captain this is helm we've passed the 1.0 light speed going to 1.6. Good. Sensors broad scan sweep please, we don't want to run into anything at this speed.

ENTERING THE
ARIOTTE SYSTEM

CAPTAIN WERE ENTERING the Ariotte system, very good helm starts to slow her down I want to come in below light speed as we get nearer. Aye sir. Plot lets see where we are relative to Cellin Yar. Aye sir, coming up on the imager. Helm bring us down to .8 light speed. Continue on course, come down ten degrees on Y axis. Aye Sir. Helm we will be entering standard orbit once we get into range. Aye sir. Sir there's one moon that will be coming up on our port side she's tucked in pretty close to the planet. Very good helm set your orbit to outside the orbit of the moon. Come down to equatorial orbit axis Aye sir. Sir we should have visual on Cellin Yar shortly. Very good sensors put it up on the screens, so everybody can see where were going. Aye sir. The screens flickered and sharpened up to show a small white light in the distance against the blackness of space.

Attention crew this is the captain speaking if you look to your nearest screen, you'll see out destination Cellin Yar in the middle. We won't be here long, only long enough to pick up the science team and then we'll be heading home. He could hear the yelling and clapping coming through the ship.

CELLIN YAR

CAPTAIN ENTERING ORBIT at Cellin Yar, very good Helm keep her steady on course keep your speed up slightly, I've noticed a strong gravitational force around the planet. Must be a lot of heavy metals here. Sir is this really an ice planet? Yes, helm I've heard it has a heavy metal core and a lot of precious metals under the ice, they mine those here and export them through out the galaxy. Sir is this place inhabited? I guess so, they have been here a long time and have adopted to the climate. Too damn cold for me though. I agree sir, I wonder what kind of people live in this place? I don't know, but we'll soon find out. I would assume that's what the science team was here for unless they were just looking at the mining structures.

Master Chief would you like to take the shuttle down and pick up our passengers? No sir I'll let the ensign go down I'm nice and warm here.

Very good then. Shuttle clear the bay when your ready. Aye Sir. Com inform the science team the shuttle is coming down and inform control they'll only be there a short time. Aye sir. Sir shuttle away. Very good control. Doctor to the shuttle bay for decontamination detail. Sir I don't think that will be a problem, I don't think anything bad can live at that temperature.

SHUTTLE BAY

CAPTAIN YOU'VE BEEN requested to the shuttle bay. The shuttle is arriving soon. Very good comm, Helm be ready to depart as soon as the shuttle gets aboard safely. Nav-set your course for home. Aye sir. Helm when I give the word break orbit and head for home, speed 1.6 light speed. Very good sir.

The shuttle bay doors were open and the landing lights from the shuttle could be seen as they set up on final approach. The decontamination tents were set up ready to receive the people. The shuttle settled in gently and the portable tunnel slid into place against the shuttle door. Soon the team started to come through the exits. The Master Chief and the Captain were waiting at the exit door to great the team. Once everyone was through the last person emerged. Her face was instantly recognizable. It was Luenia aka Anthropologist. She was radiant as ever as she scanned the crowd. When she saw The Captain, she smiled widely and walked briskly over to him. She grabbed him by the arm and pulled close on her tip toes and kissed him gently, but longley on his cheek. Good to see you again. His face betrayed his surprise and then his feelings for her. The bay doors closed and the decontamination team started to take the tents down. The science team moved off and Master Chief took them to their quarters. Luenia stayed back and walked arm and arm with The Captain. He finally said "I didn't know you were on the team. I thought you stayed back at the university." The Captain and Luenia walked to his quarters and she started to unpack her gear. I contacted HQ and asked if you were back yet and they said no you were just about to leave the Frontier. I requested you to pick us up and HQ said okay. I thought I'd surprise you.

Captain to helm-helm here sir. Set your course to home and take us out of orbit as soon as possible Aye sir course laid in and were breaking orbit now sir.

HOMEWARD BOUND

Knock on the door at the Captains quarters. Come in Master Chief. Master Chief walks in with the Captain standing in his ready room in his civilian clothes. What can I do for Chef? Well sir I thought I'd have a word with you privately. Just then Luenia appears at the sleeping chambers door. Master Chief's mouth drops open as he stars at her in her civilian clothes. Sir I didn't mean to interrupt I'll leave immediately. No chief stay where you are and let's talk. All three sit down at the table. Sir I'll come back if you prefer (it's obvious the Master Chief is very uncomfortable) nonsense Chief relax. Well sir I've come to tell you that I have decided to retire from the service as soon as we get back. The Captain and Luenia both stare at him with their mouths open. Chief what has brought this on? Sir I've thought a lot about this mission and that I find I'm just not into this stuff anymore. Before we left, I bought into a small position in the ownership of the Boar and Dragon. What are you going to do in retirement asked Luenia? Well

I contacted my partner in the Boar and Dragon and he stated he would like to get out of the business altogether. So, we struck a deal and now I'm the proud owner of that fine establishment. That's great Chief I'm truly surprised. Yes, sir I can tell after visiting with Bernardo Din and his partner Shamus I got the idea I could do the same thing minus the weapons as he did and make an emporium of fine libations. I think I would like that and have all of my friends and military people around and have a good time. That's great Chief I'm sure you'll make a fine business out of it.

Both Luenia and the Captain looked at each other and started to laugh a little. Well Chief you might as well be the first to know. Luenia and I are going to be bonded when we get back. Master Chiefs mouth just opened in shock and he started to stammer and laugh at the same time. Finely he said that's great I wish the both of you the best of luck and joy. The Captain looked at the Master Chief and said well that's not all. Master Chief I've also decided to retire when we get back, I don't think galivanting around the galaxy is way to spend one's time when they have a bonded partner at home. Sir what are you going to do.? Well that's up for discussion right now, but Luenia is taking a fulltime position at the anthropologic university.

A knock on the door. Come in says Luenia. The doctor enters the door way and is surprised to see the Captain, Luenia and Master Chief sitting at the table. OH, I'm sorry Captain I didn't know you had company I'll come back later. Nonsense Doctor come in and have a seat. Sir I just wanted to update you on my findings. Go right ahead Doctor. She sat down and looked at Luenia and the Captain dressed in casual clothing. Sir I can really come back at another time. No please Doctor go right ahead. In fact, Luenia you might be interested in my findings. Please Doctor proceed. Well first of all the results of the Autopsies of the Ferugie I examined and the cell and tissue samples I have showed that as fearsome as they seemed and acted, they were really quite fragile. Their cell structure indicated very thin cell walls. That's why they didn't live very long after being hit with the sensor beams and some minor damage from the disruptors. Sir their cells were already damaged way before we encountered them. Their cells look to have been chemically changed. Sir I think they were subjected to some type of chemical immersion. If I didn't know better, I think they were in some form of stasis for a long period of time. Doctor that could very well be true. Bernardo Din told us that they just showed up in a very strange type of craft. Then the craft disappeared and they began using the transport craft we ran into. Captain did he say anything else about them. No just that he had never seen anything like them before. That makes sense sir. I've compared their cells and structures and have found nothing even coming close to them in our galaxy. Sir I think they might have come from another galaxy, which would make my thesis of being in stasis more complete because they would need to be in stasis to travel that far. Or Doctor you might want to consider that they might even be time travelers. Do you think that's possible? Yes, I do. I've heard we've played with the idea and even done some research on the possibilities and technology needed to do it. Doctor, the frontier is a very strange place. The normal laws of physics don't seem to apply there. We slowed down once we got beyond the gravitational effects of the star systems. No known reason but it happened. The small planets we visited with the strange little methane suns in the middle of them are truly different. No place else in the galaxy do they exist, but out there they do. I think everyone of us felt odd about being out there, I even mentioned it to Master Chief. There are strange forces that we don't understand or know about at work out there. Its as if time is maybe distorted or changed. I think that's the real reason we were sent there. I think HQ wanted to send a manned expedition in there to find out what's going on. I think we were the experiment. That's very shocking Captain, but I see your reasoning.

Luenia, I would love to hear about your work on Cellin Yar some time? Well Doctor stay seated and I'll tell you. We were sent there to learn about the inhabitants on Cellin Yar and find out how we can help them.

First of all, they aren't native to Cellin Yar, they were transported there by the watchers. A race of entities that roam the universe planting different beings on planets that don't have any higher life forms. Luenia looked at the Captain and said guess where they came from? He shrugged and said I have no idea. Well they told me they came from none other than earth. They said the watchers developed them on earth to do heavy labor. They told me the watchers combined cells from the native earth creatures with theirs and then did some modifications. That's how they came about. On earth they were called the Denisovans. They still call themselves that here. The Captain just shrugged and shook his head. The watchers decided to transplant them from earth to here because they could adopt to the cold temperature and their hair fibers turn white as they grow older and get used to the cold. Initially they are a brownish color. They moved just abut all of them, but they said some were left behind to see if they could adopt to survive the many forms of higher life forms there. Interesting don't you think? These watchers, do you think they really exist? I don't know, but some of the old earth texts talk of a people that visited earth that resemble what the Denisovans describe them as. The earth people called them the Anunaki. I think there is to much similarity to be just a coincidence. The timing fits and the general physical appearance seems to as well. Well Luenia lets talk again before we get back. Captain I have to get back to the sick bay. Very good Doctor, thank you for coming up to give me an update. Your welcome sir.

Well Master Chief what do you think. Sir I think you might be right about the Ferugie and the Frontier, but I still don't' get the Ambassador traveling with us. I don't either, but Bernardo Din said that he had heard of rumors about some kind of alliance. I think that's what's going on. It might be good that he was with us. He was also feeling uneasy about the frontier. He just might go back and report that it's not a place for them.

HOME

CAPTAIN THIS IS helm. Yes helm, sir we're getting into the Ninverta system I think we should start to slow down. I agree helm, bring it back to1.0 light speed. Sir sensors indicate were getting close to Assanti. Very good bring it back to .7 light speed. Chief engineer be ready to start the pulse ion engine when we get in closer. Aye sir, it'll be good to get home. I agree Chief Engineer. I'll be leaving the bridge first officer take over, aye sir I've got the bridge.

Captain on the bridge- Captain Tallor5 enters the bridge in his dress uniform. A scarlet colored tunic, light tan pants tucked into highly polished dark brown boots. He has a gold sash around his middle and his two order of Zeus medallions hung around his neck He had his highly polished Sa attached to his sash and his birds head handle colt strapped under his left arm. He was a sight to behold as everyone stood and came to attention. At ease everyone and thank you. He took his seat. Sir we have clearance to make our final approach. Very good helm, I've got the controls.

His chair moved to the imager and his control stick came out of his chair arm rest. Sir are you going to bring us in? Yes, helm I am, since this is my last voyage, I think I should indulge myself, don't you? Very good sir you have the helm.

Docking control this is the Excalibur we'll be doing a circular final approach. Welcome home Excalibur circling approach approved. Crew this is the Captain look at your screens and you'll see the space dock coming into view. We'll be doing a circular approach so everyone can get a good look. The Excalibur slowed down and started a long circle around the immense space dock. Several ships could be seen inside including the Fang, the MaryAnne and even the old Argos. They banked around and settled into a slow controlled approach to docking bay one. In no time the ship came to a halt and the large locking arms came down and clamped on the Excalibur.

The portable entrance tunnel nudged up to the main doorway of Excalibur and shortly thereafter a noticeable hissing sound came out as the two atmospheres equalized. The Excalibur was home.

Printed in the United States
By Bookmasters